GIFTS

Laura Barnett

D1494248

WEIDENFELD & NICOLSON

First published in Great Britain in 2021 by Weidenfeld & Nicolson,
This paperback edition first published in Great Britain in 2022
by Weidenfeld & Nicolson,
an imprint of The Orion Publishing Group Ltd
Carmelite House, 50 Victoria Embankment
London EC4Y 0DZ

An Hachette UK Company

1 3 5 7 9 10 8 6 4 2

A CIP catalogue record for this book is
available from the British Library.

ISBN (Mass Market Paperback) 978 1 4746 2440 4
ISBN (eBook) 978 1 4746 2441 1
ISBN (Audio) 978 1 4746 2442 8

Typeset by Input Data Services Ltd, Somerset

Printed and bound in Great Britain by Clays Ltd, Elcograf S.p.A.

www.weidenfeldandnicolson.co.uk
www.orionbooks.co.uk

For Caleb, the greatest gift

My concern is the gift we long for, the gift that, when it comes, speaks commandingly to the soul and irresistibly moves us.

Lewis Hyde, *The Gift*

What can I give Him, poor as I am?

Christina Rossetti, 'In the Bleak Midwinter'

For Peter

She wanted to buy a gift for Peter, but could think only of mundanities. A tie, a wallet, cufflinks. A watch, but those cost a bomb if you wanted anything half-decent; otherwise, it might as well have come off a market stall. Which was a thought, actually – Maddy could trawl the market later.

The stallholders were already setting up outside, parking their vans, clanging their metal awning poles on the cobblestones. It had used to get on her nerves, all this noise three mornings a week, all this banging and shouting and the mess they left behind: the polystyrene crates with their residual fish-stink, the cabbage leaves and kale fronds and bruised apples, lying in mushy drifts around the square. Now, Maddy found it all strangely comforting: a sign, as good as any, that life had returned more or less to normal, that the world still turned.

Eight o'clock in the morning, on a Wednesday in December, in a small town close to the furthest limit of England. Chalk cliffs and downland, pebble beaches, and the testy grey reaches of the Channel. They'd gone down there in the summer, she and Peter, walked a length of the cliff path, stood staring out at the smudged layers of sun, sky, sea. 'Edge lands,' he'd said. 'They make people anxious, paranoid. Or maybe that's just me.'

She'd shrugged, smiling. 'I always feel calm out here.'

He'd looked at her. She'd felt him looking, though she hadn't turned to meet his gaze. 'You know what?' he'd said. 'I do too, right now.' And then they'd walked on.

Walking shoes, perhaps. A good pair, with cushioned soles: there had been other walks, other moments. The crisp, saline tang of the air, the wide, open sky. Peter beside her, his long, loping stride. The sadness that clung to him, slowing his pace: leading him, at times, to break off in the middle of a sentence, to drop his thread. 'Sorry, where was I?' he would say, and Maddy, beside him, would pick up the fallen skein of the conversation and hand it back. 'Here, I think. You were telling me about . . .'

But no, it was no good, was it? She didn't even know his size.

'What are you doing then, love?' Fran said. 'Made up your mind?'

Maddy took the cup Fran was offering. It was from the coffee shop across the square, the new one, the one that charged £2.50 for a flat white. She'd been planning to pop over there herself later, with a couple of the newer hardback novels: the owner, Harvey, had told her he was stumped for presents for his wife. Maddy enjoyed this: finding books to suit customers, assessing tastes. Shame she wasn't better at it when it came to her own friends, her own . . . Well. Whatever Peter was.

'Oh, that's good,' she said, gulping the coffee. 'Made up my mind about what?'

Fran had had her hair done: it was shorter, blonder, falling in neat, obedient layers across her oversized grey lambswool scarf. Her coat was black, padded, expensive. There were tiny diamonds in her ears: from Adam, Maddy presumed. He was good with gifts.

'Christmas,' Fran said. 'We've got to get our turkey order in. Today's the last day for the butcher's. You know what Adam's like . . .'

Maddy nodded: she did. He was so unapologetically himself. She liked that; envied it a little, maybe. 'Sorry to be rubbish. I'd love to come, it's just that I . . .'

'Would rather sit upstairs in your PJs watching telly?' Fran was smiling now: she had a great smile, a real high-wattage beam. 'Who wouldn't, Maddy, who wouldn't? I really don't mind – neither of us does – I just thought, after last year . . .'

Last year. Yes. All those empty weeks and months, the scored-out calendar, the shuttered shop. The call Maddy had been forced to make to Fran to say that she could no longer justify her wage, that she'd had to organise a stay of execution with the bank. She'd been lovely about it, Fran – she'd made it easy. Maddy, in her awkwardness, had been harder than she'd meant to be, almost cruel: she'd pointed out that it wasn't as if Fran had really needed the money. Cursed herself afterwards for her tactlessness, though it was true: the job had really just been an excuse for Fran to leave the house for a couple of days a week and sit chatting, arranging stacks of the prettiest hardbacks and patterned notebooks and posting her handiwork online. 'Shelf-ies', Fran called them. She still managed the social media stuff – Maddy was useless with all that – and wouldn't take a penny. She was a good friend: the best of women, really. Maddy wasn't always convinced that Adam knew quite how lucky he was.

'It's kind of you to invite me, Fran.' Maddy traced the rim of the cup with her finger. 'It's just . . .'

Just what? She was wondering what Peter was going to do for Christmas, now that Chloe was definitely going to her mum's? She wanted to hold out just a little longer, to see if he might eventually ask her the same thing? She could say none of these

3

things aloud: Fran wasn't stupid, she'd guess exactly what was going on, and Maddy didn't want to acknowledge it – not yet, not now.

Fran waved a hand. Her own coffee was still in its cardboard tray. 'No pressure, love. It'll just be the usual. Jesse's Alice might come for a bit. But there's the party, anyway. You will come to that?'

Maddy nodded. 'Of course.' Was Peter going? He knew Adam a little, had done some work for his property company: it wasn't impossible for Adam to have invited him. Maddy ached to know, but didn't dare to ask. 'I'll let you know about Christmas Day soon, Fran, I promise. And thanks.'

'Don't be silly. Chat soon.'

The silence seemed louder after Fran had gone. Wednesday mornings were quiet on the square – even now, a few weeks before Christmas – but things usually picked up around lunchtime, as the market mustered a steady dribble. Not that there was really such a thing as usual, any more. Not for Maddy, not for anyone.

Books, though: everybody needed books. Even now. Especially now.

A book for Peter, then? Too obvious; and anyway, Maddy didn't know what he'd read, or hadn't read. It was guesswork. But then it always was, giving a gift – at least, if it was a true gift, a surprise. A thing to say . . . what? Something. Something honest. Something true.

He called at lunchtime, as she was finishing her sandwich. *Al desko*, Fran called it, though this wasn't really a desk but a counter – handsome, solid oak, bequeathed, along with a pair

4

of glazed display cabinets, a mouse problem and some seriously antiquated plumbing, by the previous owner, Mr James (Maddy never could think of him as Leonard), who had run a ladies' clothing store here for half a century. He'd sold wedding hats, gloves, floral two-piece ensembles whose hemlines dipped to mid-calf. Maddy had come in quite often as a child, had sat on a satin-covered stool in the changing room out back, where Maddy now kept her stock, watching her mother, stripped to her underwear, fiddle with zips, buttons, sleeves. Straps and waistbands and the raw, marbled gleam of bare flesh. *How's this, darling? What do you think? It's fine, Mum. Can we go now? I'm bored.*

'Good day?' Peter said.

'Not bad, thanks. Yours?'

'Can't complain. Well, all right, I probably can. Spent all day wrangling the departmental budget. Come for dinner? Chloe's going out.'

That rise, that lift. Steadily, Maddy said, 'What time?'

'Shall we say eight? Give me a chance to tidy up.'

'You don't have to do that, Peter.'

'I know I don't, but I will.'

The woman who'd been lingering in the children's section – small, slim, her hair dark and cropped; a blue health worker's tunic beneath her unbuttoned coat – was approaching the counter now, carrying a pair of board books. *The Very Hungry Caterpillar. Goodnight Moon.*

'I'll have to go, Peter,' Maddy said. 'I'll see you later.'

'You will,' he said, and then he was gone.

Wine. Maddy scanned the books. She ought to take some wine tonight. A wine subscription as a gift? Too much?

'For my boys,' the dark-haired woman said. Her accent was fluid, musical. Her smile was tentative; she had the money

5

counted out in change in her palm. 'They are older, but they are learning English. So we start with the easy books.'

'Good idea,' Maddy said. 'They'll love these.' Maddy sorted the coins – not a penny short – and slipped the books into a paper bag. In her mind, all the while, she was eyeing cases of wine, and Peter's face when the box arrived at his door. That slow, shy smile, the one that tugged creases in the skin around his eyes. The call he might make to her afterwards: high, chiming cadences, sadness dispelled. *Thank you, Maddy, thank you! It's just perfect.* And it would be, wouldn't it? Perhaps it would.

They had been at school together, she and Peter – or more precisely, at adjacent schools. The boys and girls had been kept separate, even then, in the late 1970s – an era that did not, to Maddy, feel so very long ago, but whose customs seemed so quaint, so remote (no mobile phones; no internet; the girls' skirts measured with rulers if they crept too high above the knee) that it might as well have been the 1870s.

The school was co-educational now: the two grammars had conjoined, sprawling out across Lenbourne's western fringes. One of the old campuses – the boys' – had been knocked down to make way for a science and technology centre, a featureless rectangle of glass and steel. But the girls' building still stood: Maddy drove past it often, on her way to and from the out-of-town supermarket, feeling . . . What? That strange compression of time, in which she was both a fifty-six-year-old woman, driving her doddery Fiesta to Sainsbury's, and a thirteen-year-old girl in blazer and knee socks, waving to Peter at the gate.

They'd walked to school together each morning, and back again in the afternoon: Peter lived on the next street, their mothers had met at a church coffee morning. Church was another institution they had endured in parallel: long hours on hard pews, the tedium of the youth club, with the toe-curling young curate playing them the soundtrack to *Jesus Christ Superstar* on LP.

Peter, then: lanky, as he still was; shy, too, his unbrushed hair falling across his eyes, those twice-daily trudges across town often silent but for the rush and thrum of passing cars, the soft smack of school shoes on pavement. It was a long walk, half an hour each way, skirting the playing fields, taking them through the cobbled marketplace and ancillary lanes.

Occasionally, if it was very wet, or thick with snow, Peter's mother Irene drove them to school: Maddy's couldn't, she left for work at six, and her father was dead. Peter's father wasn't, but he might as well have been: he never came to church, and there was no trace of him in the car – a white Ford Cortina, kept spotless by Irene, who didn't work and chain-smoked slender, pastel-coloured cigarettes she bought in bulk in Calais twice a year. 'Maddy love,' she said when she drew up outside Maddy's house, the engine purring as Maddy locked the door with her own keys, the set she kept under her school jumper on a chain around her neck. 'Hop in.' So Maddy did, and sat on the white-leather back seat at arm's length from Peter. 'Hello,' they each said, looking away out of their respective windows at the trim terraced houses, the polished door knockers, the box hedges. Sometimes, witnessing their silence, Irene laughed, caught Maddy's eye in the rear-view mirror and said, 'You are a funny pair. Cat got your tongues?'

No, Maddy hadn't thought much of Peter then. She hadn't thought about him much at all, really, until they were fifteen and Sally Jarvis, the girl with the biggest breasts and blondest, fullest perm (her mother ran A Cut Above, the new salon on East Street), had come up to Maddy one lunchtime to ask whether she was going out with Peter Newton.

It had actually taken Maddy a second or two to realise who Sally meant. 'Peter? No.'

'Why d'you walk together, then?'

Maddy had put down her fork. 'Our mums are friends.'

Sally had stared at Maddy, hard-eyed. She'd been queen of the class back then – queen of the school, really – though you wouldn't know it now: she managed the post office in town, and didn't seem at all happy about it; just sat there behind the glass screen glowering and fiddling with her phone. Maddy had smiled at her a few times in the early months after moving back to Lenbourne, considered starting a conversation; but Sally had stared back just as blankly, offering no indication that she recognised her at all.

That day, in the lunch room, the teenage Sally had said, 'Someone I know fancies him. Find out if he's got a girlfriend, will you?'

Peter had seemed different to Maddy, somehow, after that: more substantial, his features more clearly defined. She'd told him about Sally and he'd laughed. 'Tell her I only like girls with at least half a brain.'

'I can't tell her that.'

He looked at her. They were on London Road now, almost home; it was winter, the afternoon already thickening into evening, a scarf drawn tightly around his chin. He'd had his hair cut shorter: his face, now more visible, seemed older, its contrasts starker, etched with shadow in the fading light. 'Well then,' he said, 'tell her there's someone I like.'

'Is there?'

He smiled. 'Maybe. Yes. But I don't know whether she likes me back.'

Maddy said nothing, didn't know what to say. Her mouth was dry, her heart drummed. At his corner – they reached his street before hers – Peter turned and walked off without saying good-bye and she stood stricken for a moment, watching his back. It seemed to her that an opportunity had been presented and she had missed it. There was something she should have said or done and she had failed. She had stood there on the corner, feeling the weight of that failure, until she'd had no choice but to pick up her school bag and walk on home.

He'd made chicken with chorizo, in a rich tomato sauce: he'd done most of the cooking for Laura and Chloe, he said. They were eating in the kitchen, a narrow galley lined with wood-effect units, lit by a single shadeless bulb. The table was a folding one from Ikea, squeezed between the dishwasher and the window, which looked out over the alley behind the car park, with its graffiti and its stunted weeds. The house was rented; it had been the best he'd been able to find at the time.

'Just a stopgap,' Peter had said, the first time Maddy had come round – though it had been six months now, and he and Chloe were still here.

They drank the wine Maddy had brought – a Merlot, from the Co-op on Market Square: Peter's favourite, she knew by now. When they'd finished eating they moved through to the living room – 'more space,' Peter said, and it was true, though the room wasn't, in all honesty, much less depressing. A sag-ging leather sofa (it had, like all the furniture, come with the house); an electric coal-effect fire. But there was the Christmas tree, a real one, glowing cosily in the corner. Someone – Chloe, perhaps – had made an effort with the decorations, stuffed fir off-cuts into a tall glass vase, made an artful display of pine cones and artificial berries. Her mother's daughter: the house in London had been beautiful, meticulously arranged, like something from a magazine. 'Something not quite real about it,' Owen had said, the last – the only – time they'd visited. 'It's like they're trying too hard.' Maddy had dismissed it at the time – they'd been at that stage in their marriage when it had become too easy to dismiss too much – but it seemed now that Owen had been right, as he'd been about so many things. Their ultimate unsuitability, for one thing: the fact that Maddy and Owen had each, for too many years, tried too hard to fit to the shape of the other.

Peter put on an album, a band Maddy hadn't heard of – something folky, soothing. (Music, as a gift? But no – again, how would she know what he already had, or didn't have?). At least this wasn't Christmassy; she'd had a festive playlist on in the shop all afternoon. Trade had picked up, she'd been busy, time had flown. Maddy had a soft spot for it all, really: for the lights and the glitter and the old, recycled songs. The turkey and the roast potatoes and the cracker jokes, the glorious absurdity of mongrel tradition; even, yes, if she were to spend the day alone again in her flat above the shop with a ready-made single-portion turkey crown and a bottle of gin. Last year, she'd drawn the curtains in mid-afternoon, painted her toenails gold, watched *Miracle on 34th Street* and *It's a Wonderful Life*, celebrated not having to pretend, as she'd done to Owen, that she found the old festive movies unbearably schmaltzy. It hadn't been so bad, really; but still, Maddy wasn't sure she could bear doing it all over again.

'Laura called today,' Peter said now. 'She wanted me to know that she hadn't put Chloe up to Christmas, that it was her decision.'

'Well.' Maddy gripped the stem of her wine glass. They were on the uncomfortable sofa, side by side; the choice was either to perch right on the edge of the cushions, knees angled primly away from him, or sink back, lolling against the broken springs. Maddy had opted for the former. 'That's good to know, I suppose.'

But Peter didn't seem to be listening; he had withdrawn again, shrunk back inside himself. 'I don't suppose it'll be much fun for her, for any of them. Chloe's still furious. But I guess I can see why even spending Christmas with her mother appeals more than staying in this dump with me.'

'It's not so bad,' Maddy said. This was a lie. She had been lucky, in a way: Owen had left her, there had never been any question of her moving out. She had been able to lick her wounds in the relative comfort of the little house in Beckenham that had been theirs for just six months. Until she'd sold it and slunk back to Lenbourne, leased the empty shop and the flat above; given Owen what was his by law and let him go back to his own home town: to Sheffield, with Sara, and, a year or so later, their baby girl.

'Has to be better than last year, anyway,' Peter said. 'Laura and I had a row. I can't even remember what it was about now. All our arguments just seemed to roll into one by then. The three of us spent most of the day in separate rooms.'

'Everything,' Maddy said, 'has to be better than last year.'

Peter nodded. He had turned on the fire: they watched the false coals, their lurid orange flare. The band played on: strummed guitars, drums, a chorus of male voices, layered, rising and falling. It was getting late; she'd had three glasses by now, or was it four? The walk home would be freezing: Maddy could already see herself, wrapped up, hunched against the cold, the low medieval houses of the centre dark and silent around her, all the words she should have said here, now, scrolling through her mind. *And you, Peter? What are you doing for Christmas? Are you going to Fran and Adam's party? Perhaps we could . . . Well, I thought we might . . .*

L'esprit de l'escalier. The wit of the staircase, or in Maddy's case, the cobbled street: thinking of the right words, too late. She'd read that in a novel. So much of what she knew, Maddy had read somewhere; so much of what she had experienced, too. She had lived a small life, a quiet life: away to university, to a job, a truncated marriage, a vacated home; and then back to the town in which she had grown up, whose diameter she had used to trace each day on her way to school and back, with this man – a boy, then – at her side.

Perhaps a map of Lenbourne for his Christmas gift: one of those old vintage prints, framed, with the route they used to take marked across it with a dotted line. Cute – like something a woman would do in a film. But no. That wasn't Maddy, that had never been the sort of woman she was. 'Cold,' Owen had called her, in the end. 'Cold and buttoned-up. I can't seem to get through to you, Maddy. I just can't work out how to make you *feel.*'

Maddy had finished her wine. After a while she said, 'Well, Peter, thanks so much for dinner. It was lovely. But I really should be getting home.'

He turned. He looked at her. His eyes were very blue. A moment stretched between them, taut, almost tangible. Then he cleared his throat, and broke it, looked away. 'All right. I suppose it's getting late.'

Peter's email had arrived in the spring: sent to the bookshop address, as it was a while since they'd been in touch (perhaps he'd lost her number) and Maddy had left Facebook after Owen had left her – too many photographs and memories, too much algorithmically generated pain. Peter said he was coming back to Lenbourne, too: the London house was up for sale, he and Laura were divorcing and his mother was unwell, she might have to go into a home. *Can't think of anywhere else to go*, Peter had written, and then, *Let me know if you fancy a coffee – it would be good to see a friendly face.*

Had Maddy thought of Peter much, in all that time? Not so much, really: not compared with those teenage years when Maddy's earlier indifference had turned, almost overnight, into something approaching an obsession. Scrawling his name on the inside covers of her exercise books; practising her signature with his surname as her own. That game they'd all used to play in the form room: adding up the numbers in your date of birth, then combining that with the numbers of the boy you liked, and seeing whether the outcome was auspicious. Theirs, Peter's and Maddy's, wasn't – his and Sally's, on the other hand, must have been.

One afternoon a few weeks after what Maddy had still thought of as her failure, Peter had not met Maddy at the school gate. She'd stood there, feeling foolish, singular among the plural groups of girls forming and reforming around her. After a while she'd seen them, across the road, skirting the playing field: the two of them, Sally and Peter, his arm draped loosely across her shoulders. Maddy had walked home alone; later, in her bedroom, she'd cried, until her mother, home from work, had found her, and held her, and smoothed her damp hair away from her face. 'It hurts, darling, doesn't it? I know it hurts.'

That, then, had been that: Sally-and-Peter, Peter-and-Sally, an item, a couple, for what had seemed like forever – on through the exams and into sixth form – but had only, in the end, been a couple of years. How she'd hated Sally at the time; how Maddy had cursed herself for letting Peter, as she'd seen it then, slip away.

But it had all faded eventually, as almost everything did: Maddy had almost forgotten Peter, almost forgotten all of them – the girls from school, the old Lenbourne crowd – at university, and afterwards in London. There were Facebook groups, and reunions, and Christmas Eve pub meet-ups, but Maddy rarely bothered to go. The dinner invitation had come about years later, and only because Peter had happened to come into the bookshop in Bromley one afternoon.

Maddy had been at the counter, placing an order. 'I wonder,' she'd heard a man say, 'if you could help me choose a present for my wife. It's her birthday, you see, and she loves . . . Maddy Connell, is that you?'

She'd looked up from the computer and seen him: Peter Newton. A man now, of course, married, with a child, and living not far away, in Crystal Palace: they'd done the chit-chat, filled in the blanks, until a small queue had begun to form behind him. So he'd taken her number, said she – *they*, Maddy and Owen – must come to dinner. And had actually arranged it, too, which Maddy hadn't expected. But the evening hadn't been easy: a Tuesday, reheated lasagne and supermarket salad; Laura, copper-haired, milk-skinned, polite but distant, disappearing more than once to answer her mobile in another room.

'Corporate law,' Peter had said. 'You know how it is.'

They didn't know, she and Owen – she'd worked in book-shops since graduation; he was a software engineer – but they'd nodded politely, sipped their wine. And if Maddy had thought about the evening much at all since then, it was only to reflect that Owen had been right: Laura and Peter had been trying too hard, or perhaps nowhere near hard enough.

So yes – what had happened next had come as a surprise. The coffee, a few weeks after Peter's email, on a Monday afternoon (Maddy's only regular day off since having to let Fran go) at Jackson's, the converted brewery down by the creek. Maddy's suggestion: she liked the place, sometimes went there for lunch on Mondays, just sitting and reading and watching the water, the reeds and the mudbanks and the tidal ebb. She'd been sitting there, at her usual table, when she'd heard her name, looked up – and there he had been again, Peter, older and sadder and shabbier but still there, still *him*. She had blinked and stared, and it had been like that moment in the optician's chair, when the blurred test-lens was removed and the world looked back, clear and sharp and perfectly in focus. *Oh, it's you. Hello.*

On Saturday, Maddy ordered it: typed the word into Google on a whim, chose the first one she could find. Time was running out, after all: just days to go till Christmas. The gift might not arrive in time, or at all, but at least she'd done it: at least she'd made a choice.

A telescope: not too expensive, not too cheap. The thought had come that morning, in the shower, and stayed with her as she'd made coffee and toast, the market traders setting up again on the square below. Peter loved the night skies out here, had said more than once that he'd forgotten what it was like to be able to see the stars. It was a good present, Maddy thought – or if it wasn't, no matter; it was done.

His texts came in the afternoon: she'd been out in the stock-room, unloading a delivery, had left her phone on the counter.

Peter's name was there when she retrieved it. Her pulse accelerating, the sudden rush and skip. Ridiculous. She was too old for this; she was just too old. And yet.

Maddy put down the phone, went over to the door, turned the sign to 'Open'. Came back to the counter, and then, only then, picked up her phone, read the first of his messages.

Maddy – thanks so much for coming the other night. You cheered me up, as always. Sorry if I droned on. Look, I wanted to ask you something. I've got a table at the Plough for Christmas lunch – they've had a cancellation, and I was on the list, had been thinking of taking Chloe. I can't face eating on my own. Come with me, would you, if you're free? My treat. P x.

And then the second message, sent a few minutes later.

PS OK, I'll be honest. It's not that I can't face eating on my own.

And the third, a minute or two after that.

PPS OK, maybe this is too much. But here goes. There's this party on the 23rd. Fran and Adam Lytton. Fran's a friend of yours, isn't she? Fancy going together?

Maddy smiled at no one, there in the empty shop, and then tapped out her reply. *Yes, Peter. Yes to it all.*

For Chloe

Peter remembered so clearly the day that Chloe was born. Of course he did – he was her father – though he hadn't understood this, not really, until the moment she'd emerged from her mother, blood-smeared, bluish and wrinkled, a soft fruit left too long in the sun.

No cry had come from her for the longest time. Activity in the operating theatre had sharpened, redoubled. Machines beeping, masks and scrubs, the bright, bright lights. Peter had stood redundantly, holding Laura's hand; her cheeks were wet, and he'd reached across to dry them with his fingers. 'Where is she?' Laura said. 'Why isn't she crying? Why can't I hold her?'

Nobody replied: they were busy, all of them, a flock of blue-gowned birds with their daughter at its centre. He held Laura's hand, and his breath, and after a long, long moment, finally it came: the cry, a ragged bleat. The flock scattered and regrouped. Peter let go of his breath. Someone – the paediatrician, perhaps; he had forgotten all their names, would not remember their faces either, though at the time he'd thought they would stay forever imprinted on his brain – came over to the operating table with Chloe in her arms. A mewling bundle in a hand-knitted hat and the blanket they'd brought from home: white merino wool, an absurd choice, now daubed with unidentifiable rust-coloured smears.

'Your daughter,' the faceless doctor said. 'You can hold her for a moment, Laura, try to feed her if you like, and then we'll have to take her upstairs. She's doing OK, but she's going to need a bit of special care, all right?'

All right: what could possibly have been *all right* about any of this? But he'd nodded, he'd tried to smile. Peter was crying now, too. His daughter, cradled against her mother's chest, between the wires and the sticking plasters and the loosened neckline of her hospital gown. The little woollen hat, its red bobble, a cherry on a cake. Chloe's tiny mouth, opening and closing, giving out its high, kittenish wail. The tight-drawn slits of her eyes.

He'd placed a hand to the bulb of her head and felt the warmth of it through the wool, the pulse of her blood, the fragile armature of her skull. *My daughter. My child.* One hand still in Laura's, the other cradling their daughter's head: the three of them, together for a moment before the blue-gowned birds had carried the child away.

'What would you like, then, Chloe?' he said.

She didn't look up: her head was bowed over her phone, she was texting as she ate, shovelling oats into her mouth. Nightly, she made this strange concoction, oats soaked in yoghurt with honey and dried berries she ordered in bulk online, spending more than Peter did on several bottles of wine. Sometimes Chloe didn't finish her morning jar, and then it sat there on the top shelf of the fridge, multiplying, spawning replicas of itself, until the ones at the back started to bloom with mould, and then it was he – *he* – who had to throw the whole lot away, scraping the clagged contents into the food waste bin, scrubbing the insides of the jars. He'd tried to speak to her about it, but she just gave him a look and turned away; reminding him so much, in those moments, of Laura that Peter ended up turning away also, saying nothing, for fear of betraying a frustration that wasn't, of course, really Chloe's to receive.

'Like?' she said.

Peter shifted his gaze to the window: the car park, the un-emptied bins, the low wall with its amateurish graffiti – *sok*, one tag read, gnomically. He took a breath. *Breathe*, the nasal Californian on his meditation app told him daily. *Breathe, and feel yourself drawing towards the centre line.* What, he always wanted to snap back, with a most unmeditative frustration, is a centre line? I'm not a bloody Tube train.

'For Christmas, Chloe. What would you like for Christmas?'

She looked up then, offered him her slow-lidded, brown-eyed gaze. Her mother's eyes. His own frown, on his daughter's face, now softening into a smile. 'Sorry, Dad. I said I'd do a list, didn't I? I'll send you a few things today. Promise.'

Peter smiled back. What a miracle she was, sitting there in her pyjamas, eating her oats, holding her phone, connecting neuron to synapse; what a bright, shining miracle. It always came back to that, didn't it? Always, it came back to that.

'Be great if you could, Chlo. It's not long now, and the deliveries are up shit creek. Queues at Dover. The same old story.' She said nothing; she had returned her attention to the glow of her screen. He stood, carried his plate and cup to the sink; rinsed and sluiced, left them upturned on the draining board. Well trained, he supposed he was, though of course it was reductive to think of men – of himself – as needing training. He wasn't his father, either: Laura had never had to hassle him to help. He'd done most of it: the cooking, the washing, the cleaning (well, when Patricia was unwell, or on holiday, and couldn't do her four hours a week). Laziness, at least, had never been a source of Laura's complaints.

'Which day are you leaving for London again, Chlo?'

'Christmas Eve, Dad. I already told you. The day after the party. I'll take the train.'

He leant back against the worktop (marble-effect plastic, ugly as hell, like the whole house), watching her. The reddish hair she hardly ever brushed, drawn into a careless knot at the nape of her neck. The long curve of that neck, curled like a question mark over the table, the phone. Which party did she mean? Oh yes, the Lyttons'; she was meant to be waitressing: one of the other girls at the café had asked if she wanted to earn a bit of extra cash. Peter had been invited, actually – Lenbourne was a small town, not so many parties to go round, and he'd done some work with Adam Lytton. He hadn't decided yet whether to go: it would be odd, perhaps, for Chloe to have her dad there as a guest while she was handing round canapés.

The curve straightened, became a line: Chloe looked at him again and said, 'You will be all right without me, Dad, won't you?'

Peter nodded. 'Of course, sweetheart. I'll be just fine.'

He would be, surely he would. He was on the waiting list for a table at the Plough: he'd wanted to take Chloe – a treat to celebrate the end of a truly awful year – but, as with everything, he'd left it too late, and they had no space. It didn't matter anyway, now that Chloe was going home for Christmas. *Home*: he couldn't help it, that was still how he thought of the house in Crystal Palace, though none of them actually lived there any more. Not even Laura. There were strangers, now, in the house that had been home for twenty years.

'Well. I suppose I'd better get to work.'

'All right, Dad.' Chloe was back fiddling with her phone; honestly, it was as if it had been surgically attached. 'See you at lunch, then, maybe, yeah?'

The departmental meeting overran, as it usually did: there was always somebody, droning on about something, hijacking the agenda, indifferent to the growing restlessness of his colleagues (it was almost always a he). At least it was easier to ignore them on Zoom than it had been when he still worked in the office. Peter minimised the window and carried on rummaging around online, trying to find something for Chloe. A surprise: but what on earth would she like? Trainers, perhaps – she did wear those – though would she really like those enormous clodhopping soles, and anyway, what was her size? He'd have to go hunting about in her wardrobe, and he didn't fancy that: who knew what he might find? Jewellery, then: he liked the idea of that, a father choosing a necklace for his almost grown-up daughter. Something tasteful, discreetly expensive, like this rose-gold bee. He checked the price, swallowed: who was he kidding?

His name echoed from his laptop speakers: he closed the jewellery website, returned to Zoom. The meeting was staggering to its end. 'Great, then, that's a plan,' Peter said. 'Let's regroup in the new year.' He slammed his laptop shut and rushed downstairs, hoping to catch Chloe, but she'd already gone out, leaving a bowl of soup for him with a plate over it and a note. *Back for dinner, Dad. C.*

She hadn't said what she was doing this afternoon or with whom. He ought to know: perhaps Laura was right, he was useless at keeping track of their daughter's comings and goings.

But she was eighteen now – old enough, he thought, to have a longer leash; longer, anyway, than the one Laura allowed her. And if he called her to ask, he'd get some vague, evasive answer ('Just out with a friend, Dad, all right?'): Chloe hated being held to account, just as Laura always had. 'You're so *smothering*,' Laura had said once, towards the end, when she'd been late back from work for the fifth night in a row and he'd been sitting there waiting for her at the kitchen table, her dinner overcooking on a low oven, like some pathetic bearded version of a 1950s housewife. Even his mother had had more dignity: at least, in the face of his father's long unexplained absences, Irene had enjoyed herself, had had her friends round, had sat with them at the dining table under the low, green-shaded lamp. Playing cards, laughing; a record on, the smoke from their cigarettes curling up towards the ceiling and hanging there, suspended, like fine wisps of fog.

His mother. Irene. It was almost two o'clock, and he'd said he'd be round at three: if he ate quickly, there'd be time for a quick trawl around Market Square. There was that new home-wares place – perhaps he'd find something for Chloe in there – and he could pop in to see Maddy in the bookshop. Peter took a spoon from the drawer, carried the cooling soup over to the table. Perhaps Maddy would be able to help him with this absurd pretence that he knew his daughter: that he had any idea at all about what Chloe wanted, or thought, or felt. And if Maddy couldn't, no matter: just seeing her would lift his mood.

Chloe's decision to come with him to Lenbourne had taken all of them by surprise: Laura, Peter, perhaps even Chloe herself.

She'd mentioned it for the first time casually, over breakfast, which Laura was insisting on them all having together at the kitchen table – the three of them, even on weekdays, even though they were no longer a proper family (he was *leaving*, for God's sake, the house was up for sale). They'd been eating their toast (Peter), granola (Laura) and Weetabix (Chloe, who hadn't yet discovered the oat thing), the radio droning away in the background, when she'd come out with it, blithe and offhand, as if she'd been offering some comment on the news.

'Dad,' she said, 'I'm going to come with you.'

Laura put down her spoon.

'Come with me where?' Peter said, stupidly: he knew she didn't mean to Waitrose.

'To Lenbourne, of course.' Chloe took another mouthful of cereal; from across the table they watched her, her mother and father, in equal silent astonishment. Mildly, Chloe added, 'If you're moving out, Dad, then so am I.'

Peter had seen Laura angry before – they were divorcing, weren't they? – but that morning, things had gone to another level. She hadn't shouted, or thrown things – not at first – but her cheeks had sprouted a deep-red rash, and her voice had taken on that low, husky, measured quality that, in their early days, he'd found impossibly sexy, even when she was telling him in no uncertain terms to fuck off.

'No, Chloe, you're not. Don't be ridiculous. You're seventeen years old. You have your A-levels, for God's sake – I don't care that the exams have been cancelled, you've still got a hell of a lot of work to do. And then university. You'll be leaving home *then*. You're not going anywhere *now*.'

Chloe had turned to her mother, said coolly, 'I don't think you're in a position to lecture me on what I should and shouldn't do, Mum, do you?' And then it had begun: the door-slamming and the shouting and the calling of names, a whole string of them, hard-vowelled insults Peter had hardly imagined their quiet, studious daughter even knew (yes, she was seventeen, but in his mind she was still about four, pouring imaginary cups of tea for Peppa Pig).

Peter had hung back, unsure what role to play: it *was* ridiculous, of course Chloe couldn't come with him, he hadn't even sorted out anywhere to live yet, and wasn't she off to Brighton in a few months anyway, all being well? But on the other hand . . . Well, Chloe had chosen him, hadn't she? She was taking his side, and for that, naturally, he was grateful. Amazed, even: he'd felt, ever since Chloe was little, if not invisible to her, then a little smudged – a blurred photocopy, compared with the clear, high-focus image of her mother. A lieutenant, perhaps, to Laura's captain. Which was a part of the problem, it seemed, as Laura saw it: his passivity, his reluctance to take charge. For this, and more, she was ending their marriage, calling time.

'You're enjoying this,' Laura had spat at him that morning before she'd left for the office: she'd had to go, she was due in at half past nine, and Laura was never late, never absent, even if the world was imploding around her. When it *had* imploded, in fact – the virus, the chaos, the panic – she'd still insisted on going in, masked and gloved on an empty train, until the senior partners had voted to close the office doors. 'You've put her up to it. Turning her against me. My own daughter.'

Peter had found his tongue then, still sitting there at the kitchen table, his tea cold, his toast unfinished. 'My daughter too, Laura. And for God's sake, if she's angry with you, it's because you've decided to break her family apart.'

Laura had looked at him for a long moment, dignified in her navy wool coat, her eyes brown and fierce, her red hair loose across her shoulders. A part of him had still loved her then, despite it all: still found her beautiful, still wanted her. Pathetic, he supposed; but perhaps she had felt it too – the weight of their history, of the people they had been, the daughter that still bound them. For she had turned suddenly gentle, wistful even, and said, 'Peter. I have to go. Just please, for once in your life, talk to her, will you? Tell her this isn't going to work. She must see that. She must.' And then she'd turned and clipped off down the hallway and out the door, leaving him alone with the breakfast things, and the radio, and their almost-adult child still stomping around upstairs.

His mother's flat smelt of oranges and cloves: she was mulling wine when he arrived, stirring a pot at the stove. Carols on the radio, her other hand waving a cigarette like a conductor's baton. The sight cheered him, chimed with his mood, with the sense of lightness that seemed to follow any time he spent with Maddy. Lovely Maddy, with her fringe and her dresses and her fine, intelligent eyes. She knew Fran, didn't she, Adam Lytton's wife? It struck him now to wonder whether she was going to the Lyttons' party, and how he might find out.

'Mother,' he said, 'it's three in the afternoon.'

Irene turned, nodded, offered her cheek for a kiss. Her apron had a black cat on it, apparently stirring a mug of tea with its paw. The words *I Do What I Want* were stamped in fat black letters underneath.

'Half past,' she said. 'You're late.'

'I stopped at the bookshop on the way. Chloe won't tell me what she wants for Christmas. I'm stumped. Is that new?'

She was stirring the pot again now; steam rose from it, boozy and fragrant. 'What?'

'The apron.'

Irene nodded again. 'Alina,' she said, drawing two mugs from a cupboard. When he said nothing, she added, 'You know. Alina. My carer. An early Christmas present. I gave her one, too. Smellies from Boots – nice ones. We opened them yesterday. We didn't want to wait. We had tea and some of those mince pies you brought.'

'Oh.' Alina. Peter could muster only a vague image to accompany the name – small, slim, rather attractive, as he recalled, in a dark, pixie-ish way. 'That's nice.'

'It was. Here. Drink. Sit.' She handed him a mug, and he followed her obediently through to the living room. Tinsel around every picture, the plastic tree he remembered from his childhood – it had to be almost as old as him – blinking red and green and gold from its foil-wrapped plinth beside the television. Nicer than his, for all Chloe's efforts. The whole place, small as it was – and in a sheltered housing block, for goodness' sake – was nicer than his. What was he doing there, in that ugly little terraced house, in the town in which he'd been born; what were they doing, he and Chloe? He should speak to her, sit her down, persuade her to return to London, stay on with her mother into the new year. School was done with now; she was supposed to be working somewhere more exciting, career-developing, than the coffee shop on Market Square: taking courses, doing something to justify the concept of a gap year. This had been a condition of her mother's eventual acceptance of Chloe's rebellion, one fought on several fronts: delaying university (Chloe had won her place to read psychology at Sussex, now deferred), upping sticks from London to Kent.

Laura was right: he just wasn't up to solo parenting. He couldn't even work out what to buy Chloe for Christmas. 'Does she read novels?' Maddy had asked him earlier, smiling at him in that way she did, that way that made him feel calmer, steadier:

a life raft, a buoy. Better than any meditation app. They'd been friends at school, or almost-friends: their mothers had known each other from church. He'd hardly remembered Maddy, not really, and now here she was, here they both were, in late middle age, washed up again in their home town. 'Which writers does she like?'

He'd frowned, attempting to picture Chloe's expansive bedroom in London, the built-in bookshelves, neatly lined with out-turned spines; Chloe was tidy and ordered like her mother, and yes, she did read, though he couldn't for the life of him think of the name of a single author on those shelves. Austen? Dickens? J.K. Rowling? Peter didn't read much himself, not much other than business reports and sports news and gig reviews; he was ashamed to admit it, especially to Maddy, but it was true.

'A camera,' Irene said now, sipping her mug of wine, lifting berry-stained lips from its rim. 'Chloe wants a camera. A proper one, you know, with one of those lenses that extends. A zoom lens.'

He stared at her. 'How do you . . . ?'

Irene shrugged. 'We talk. I listen.'

He took a gulp of wine, let it slip, spiced, warming, down his throat. 'I listen to her.'

'No you don't. Not really. Neither of you do.'

Peter drew a breath, counted. *One*, said the nasal Californian. *Two. Three.* 'What is Chloe saying' – he spoke slowly, carefully – 'that we're not hearing?'

Irene shifted on her chair, fixed him with her long-nosed, beakish gaze. She was handsome in her dotage, white-haired, pale and winnowed as driftwood; straight-backed, almost regal. Fashion still preoccupied her, even if its precepts, for her, were those of an earlier, more formal, age. The apron was an aberration (she must really like this carer); under it she was wearing a wool twinset, ivory Angora, and a knee-length skirt of green tweed. Peter knew that the worst things for his mother, in the hospital, had been the gowns, indecorously gaping at the back, and the inability to wash her own hair: he'd done it for her, leaning her head gently back over the basin, and brought her best dressing gown and slippers from home. Irene had still been in the old house then: Nelson Street, one street away from Maddy, or Maddy as she'd once been – a child, like him, both of them younger than Chloe. All the old places; all the gaps in memory, all the spaces they had left behind.

'Where,' Irene said, 'do you think Chloe is right now?'

Peter set his mug down on the table beside him, a little too hard, sending a small spatter of wine across the cover of the festive edition of the *Radio Times*. 'Sorry,' he said. 'But, come on, Mum. Don't talk in riddles. What are you trying to say?'

Irene pursed her lips, took another long swig from her mug. Really, she was infuriating; he ought to have chucked her in a home, left her there to moulder, not moved fifty miles out of London the better to see to her care . . . Oh, better to be honest, he'd had nowhere else to go: nowhere, at any rate, that he could afford on his reduced divorcé's budget (and it wasn't as if he did that much for his mother anyway, really, other than pop by a couple of times a week; the carers saw to all the rest).

'Don't worry,' Irene said. 'Chloe's fine. Well, more or less. Ask her, Peter. Talk to her. You're her father. It really isn't my story to tell.'

Peter suggested they went for a walk the following afternoon; he didn't have much in the diary, everyone was winding down for Christmas, and Chloe was on the morning shift (this, at least, he knew). He met her outside the café. Black-painted sign, gold trim, the daily roast chalked on a blackboard. His daughter seemed diminished, seen from a distance, standing on the pavement in her coat, hat and scarf: a padded bundle, armed against the cold. That swaddled newborn, opening and closing her tiny mouth. That toddler, stumbling in puddle-suit and wellington boots; that small girl, quiet and watchful, in her hat and mittens, staring back at him impassively as he pushed her on the swings.

'Have you eaten?' he said as he approached. 'Want to get something on the way?'

Chloe shook her head. 'I had a panini.'

'All right then. Let's go.'

They crossed the square, took Church Street, following the cobbles down past the huddled Elizabethan terraces, with their struts and gables and hand-decorated wreaths, to follow the course of the creek. The town fell away quickly: the last straggling buildings – his favourite, the Captain's House, once neglected, almost derelict, now renovated, clad in tasteful white and grey – gave way to mudbanks, reeds, the high, anguished yelp of gulls. It was milder than it had been in recent days: the wind had dropped, the sky lay heavily, a dirty off-white, like sullied snow.

'Chloe,' he said eventually, reluctantly breaking a silence he'd been enjoying, interpreting as easy, even companionable. 'Are you OK? Grandma said . . .'

She turned her head sharply. 'What did Grandma say?'

Fear tugged at his gut: what did his mother know? 'Nothing, really. Just that I should talk to you. That perhaps I wasn't . . . listening. To whatever it was you might need, or want, to say.'

'Oh.'

Silence again: not easy now, but fraught, charged. Peter cleared his throat. 'I know I'm not always the best at . . . well, communicating. God knows, your mother made that clear enough.'

'Dad, don't.'

'Sorry.' He was. They walked on. Damn it, why was he so bloody useless at doing what seemed to come so naturally to everyone else? Asking questions, opening up. It had driven Laura to distraction, and now he couldn't find a way to tell Maddy how he was starting to feel about her – even to frame it for himself, in his own mind – and far worse, his daughter was in some kind of trouble, and he was making a hash of it all. Terrible images flashed through his mind, drawn from news stories and late-night TV documentaries: sex trafficking, grooming, predatory older men. Was that why she'd wanted to make a getaway from London, why she'd decided to spend a year down here with him, in a town where all that passed for nightlife was a handful of ancient pubs hosting quizzes and occasionally sending generally amiable drunkards spilling out on to the street? Was Chloe fleeing some sort of tragedy, some sort of . . . whisper it; no, Peter couldn't even do that, not aloud . . . *abuse*?

'There was someone,' she said, her face angled away from him, her voice trailing off towards the estuary, the silver, receding sea. 'There was someone I loved, and now there isn't.'

Headlines still swirled in his mind; his mouth was dry. 'Someone? Who? A man? How old?'

She looked at him, disdainful. 'Dad. For God's sake. A man, yes – or a boy. I don't know. Well, I mean, I do. His name's Jas. Jasper. He's nineteen. At uni now. Glasgow. Miles away.'

The relief: Peter was giddy with it, floating. Jasper! Nineteen! Thank God! Shout the boy's name from the rooftops! He gathered himself. He breathed. 'Jasper? You never mentioned a

30

Jasper. Was he at school? The year above? Does your mum know about him?'

Chloe shook her head. Beside him, she seemed to shrink a little, draw her neck down further into her scarf. 'Nobody knew about him. About us, I mean. Not really. I didn't tell anyone. He had a . . .' The ellipsis hung for a moment, and he let it, fought the urge to fill the gap. 'A girlfriend, Dad. He still does. In fact, she's his fiancée now.'

'Oh, Chlo.' They had reached a fork in the path: left along the coastal trail, deeper into the marshes and the mud; right to loop back towards Lenbourne. They stopped. He faced her, put his hand on her arm. Her cheeks were flushed, her eyes damp. She wouldn't meet his gaze.

'I was with him yesterday,' she said. 'Jas came to see me here. He's back in London for Christmas. He kept messaging me. I thought he was going to end it with her. I thought we were . . .' She lifted her face, looked at him. Tears were coursing down her cheeks. 'Special, I guess. I'm an idiot. The worst kind. I hate myself, what I did. I . . .'

'Chloe. Darling. Come here.' He opened his arms and she stepped into them, and they stood there, wrapped around one another, alone among the reeds and the gulls, under the low December sky.

He found the camera on eBay: a decent one, he thought, a Nikon, five years old but in full working order, sold by a reput- able second-hand shop in Bristol. It was the landscape around Lenbourne, she'd explained, that had made her think seriously about photography: the marshlands, the estuary, the widescreen sky. She'd been taking photos on her phone, but it wasn't the same. There was a digital photography course she was thinking of taking next year, at that adult education college in Holborn: yes, it might make more sense for her to stay on with her mother in London after Christmas, at least for a bit; she could always come back if he was lonely.

'Is that why you came with me, Chlo?' he'd said; they'd been having dinner, fish and chips from the good place on the Canterbury Road. 'Because you were worried I'd be lonely?'

'Maybe a bit.' Chloe squinted at him over her paper bag, holding her wooden fork: they hadn't bothered with plates, or even proper cutlery. Sachets of ketchup and tartare sauce, and the incomparable mingled tang of vinegar and oil and salt. 'I mean, who'd want you now, decrepit as you are?' She smiled. 'But no, really I just wanted to get away. Be somewhere different, you know?'

'I do.'

They were silent for a bit, eating, and then Peter said, 'Call your mum tonight, Chloe, eh? Tell her what's been going on. She needs to know. She'll want to know.'

'All right. Yeah, I guess I should.'

She had. And he'd talked to her the next day, Laura; she'd called him on her mobile, said she was walking along Central Hill. He'd imagined her, striding through their old neighbourhood (with customary good fortune, she'd managed to find a renovated loft apartment not far from the house they'd sold), and felt . . . nothing, not really. Laura's features, in his mind, seemed blurred, indistinct; the only faces he could really picture clearly in that moment, he realised, were his daughter's and Maddy's. He'd heard back from the Plough. There'd been a cancellation for Christmas Day. A table for two. He was going to text Maddy later, invite her, to that and to the party: sod it all, he had to open his mouth and speak.

'She's all right, though, do you think?' Laura had asked him on the phone, with a deference that was unfamiliar to him, untested.

'She is. She is. Or she will be, anyway.'

There was music at Laura's end of the line: he caught tinny snatches of it, guitars and drums and phoney celestial bells. 'Santa Claus Is Coming to Town'. 'OK, Peter. Well, you did well in getting her to open up. God knows, Chloe's a closed book sometimes.'

'Aren't we all.'

Laura gave a small, brittle laugh. 'Yes. Well. I'd better go, I'm meeting Kate for brunch at Brown and Green. I'm outside now. I'll see Chloe on Christmas Eve. And Peter . . .'

'What?'

'Have a good Christmas, if we don't speak before. I hope it's . . . Well. I hope it's restful, or whatever you need it to be.'

'Thanks, Laura. You too.' And then she was gone, the phone silent, and he was back on eBay, ordering the camera: the perfect one, the one he would wrap and watch his daughter opening, smiling, looking up at him as if in response to words only the two of them could hear.

For Irene

Once, when they were in bed – curled on Jas's futon, which was tucked right under the eaves, so that if you sat up too quickly you were at risk of banging your head on the ceiling – he had asked her who or what she loved most in the world. She had toyed with saying it was him – if only to see his face – but had demurred, concerned that he'd know she was only making a joke out of the truth.

'My grandmother,' Chloe said, realising, as she did so, that this was also true. 'My dad's mum. Irene.'

'Tell me about her.'

Jas shifted on to his side. He was naked, as she was; his skin was perfect, smooth, the only flaw a small scar over his breastbone (a keyhole operation back in Iran, when he was five: he had almost died). He was far better-looking than she was; Chloe knew it, though Jas didn't seem to. He said her pale skin was nacreous, like the inside of a shell (he was very clever, too: he'd applied to read English at Glasgow – would have put down Cambridge, if he hadn't wanted to piss off his parents so much). He liked to bury his face in her hair, inhale its scent; he said red hair smelt different to other shades. He called her Fox Girl, or Foxy, or Little Fox. Her name was in his phone as *LF*. Couldn't be down as Chloe, after all, or Esme

35

would notice her messages; there'd been a couple of close calls, though Jas swore he deleted everything she sent as soon as it arrived. All those words, sent out into the ether, little vanishing vapour trails.

Chloe was on her back, facing the slope of the roof; she lifted an arm, brushed the paintwork with her hand. He'd pinned pictures there, above the bed – not porn, or chintzy holiday postcards (who sent those these days, anyway?), but images of artworks: an abstract blue figure by Matisse, a black-and-white photograph of the painter Georgia O'Keeffe as an old woman – a spare, austere figure turned away from the camera, as if lost in her own thoughts. Perhaps there was something about her that reminded Chloe of Irene; perhaps that was why her grandmother had sprung so readily to mind.

'She's ninety-two,' Chloe said, 'and super-skinny, and smokes like a chimney. Cares a lot about clothes – like, *really* cares. She has this amazing fur coat from the 1960s – real fur, I mean I know it's awful and we're supposed to hate it, but she looks amazing in it, like a film star. Audrey Hepburn, or someone.'

Jas caught her hand where it was resting, palm flat against the ceiling. Meshed his fingers with hers. 'And you love her more than your mum and dad?'

Guilt clawed at her throat – was that wrong? Was it even true? But she was used to guilt, by then. 'Maybe. At the moment. They're a fucking nightmare right now. Fighting all the time. My mum hates my dad, basically – has done for years. And Grandma, she's . . .'

'What?'

'So strong. Her husband was awful to her – verbally abusive, mainly. Physically, too, I think. She has these scars. Nobody talks about it. And he had affairs.'

Jas's grip tightened on her hand. Perhaps he didn't even notice; he didn't seem to care about their situation as much as she did. He didn't talk much about Esme, but when he did, it was as if he were speaking about a distant family friend. She was his second cousin; his mother had introduced them. It wasn't *arranged*, exactly – this wasn't Tehran; his mother ran her own cosmetics brand, had an MBA – but there was what Jas called an 'understanding'. The only trouble was that Chloe didn't understand it, not one bit: not least the fact that he was prepared to defy his parents on almost everything except this.

Chloe said, 'Grandma chucked him out after my dad and uncle had gone to uni. She's tough as anything, even though she's sick right now. Really sick. She won't take any crap from the doctors and nurses. From anyone.'

'Shit.' Jas placed his other hand to her chin, cupped it for a moment, let go. 'I'm sorry she's sick.'

Chloe nodded. She was still staring at the ceiling. The paint was pale-grey, expensive, like everything in Jas's house. Her mum would have approved, if only she knew. If only she could know. 'Yeah. Me too.'

Chloe had found her grandmother's Christmas present in the summer, on a trip to the V&A: a pair of silk pyjamas, white and blue, in a swirling William Morris pattern. They'd cost £70: a fortune, really, far more than Chloe could afford to spend. But Lina, who'd suggested they go – her mum was a member, so they'd gone around all the exhibitions for free – got a discount in the shop, so that had helped. And she hadn't been able to resist them: she could see Irene wearing them, elegant with her silvery hair, the lipstick she still wore most days, even in the hospital, even when she hadn't had a mirror with her to check it. That had broken Chloe's heart more than anything, really: to see her grandmother there on the ward, propped up against thin white pillows, her lipstick dragged uneasily across her mouth, a clown's smudged smile.

Anyway, she'd been discharged by then; there'd been talk of a home – horrifying – but Irene seemed to have rallied, mustered her considerable strength. A compromise had been struck (Chloe had heard her dad on the phone for what seemed like hours, talking to her uncle Richard, to care services, to the council, the GP): the house on Nelson Street was to be sold, a flat bought in a sheltered housing block in the centre of town. It wasn't a bad place. You could see the old Jackson's brewery from Irene's bedroom window – even, if you pressed your face right against the glass, a patch of creek water, or more often black, silted mud: the tide in Lenbourne always seemed to be out, as if even the river grew bored and restless after a few hours in the town.

No, that was unfair: Chloe liked Lenbourne, always had. More than London, in some ways, especially as a child: then, she'd enjoyed the smallness of the place, its knowability. In London there was always some new corner you hadn't explored, even in an area you'd lived in all your life – Lenbourne she could map in her mind, walk its haphazard grid of streets and alleyways, though really the town was changing too. There were several new housing estates on the fringes, out by Sainsbury's, by her dad's old school; most of the old houses in the centre had been renovated, spruced up. Some seriously cool new shops – the homewares place on Market Square was quite big on Instagram, and there was a really good bookshop, run by a woman called Maddy, who had apparently been at school with Dad. Chloe remembered, vaguely, the woman coming to dinner one night years ago, with a husband in tow: a mild-mannered, rabbity guy, quiet, reserved. Chloe didn't mind that – she was on the shy side herself, understood the draw of silence. The husband was long gone; Maddy liked Chloe's dad, *liked* him, it was obvious to anyone with half a brain. Chloe suspected that her dad liked Maddy, too, and she hadn't quite decided how she felt about it, not yet. Perhaps he hadn't either.

She was examining the silk pyjamas now; they were still in their plastic wrapping, she'd taken them out from under the bed, along with the other gifts she'd bought so far. Books mainly, selected with Maddy's help: a big coffee-table thing for her mum, on interior design; a new history of the Labour Party for her uncle Richard; a Mediterranean cookbook for her other grandma, her mum's mum, over in Dorset: they were both alone now, the two grandmothers, but only Irene's solitude had been a choice. Grandma Hazel had adored her husband, Bill, whom Chloe had called Grandpa, though they hadn't actually been related: he'd been Hazel's second husband; her first – Laura's father – had died when Laura was six. Bill had fallen to the virus, the first wave; the family hadn't been able to attend the funeral. He'd been a kind man, jovial, heavyset: Chloe had loved him, too, as she did Grandma Hazel. But it was true, what she'd told Jas that day: it was Grandma Irene she loved most of all.

'Sod him,' Irene had said when Chloe told her that Jas was getting engaged, that Esme's parents didn't want them both off at different universities without having formalised their promise. 'Sod him and the horse he rode in on.'

'What?' Chloe stared at her grandmother; they were in Irene's living room, drinking gin and tonics, eating anchovy-stuffed olives from the deli on Church Street. As far as Chloe could tell, Irene appeared to consume nothing other than cigarettes, alcohol and assorted tinned delicacies – stuffed vine leaves, artichokes, sardines in tomato sauce. 'What does that even mean?'

'It means' – Irene leant forward, conspiratorial, tapping the ash from her cigarette into her ancient tobacco tin – 'that he's a fool, Chloe. A bloody fool.'

'Grandma!' Chloe had hardly ever heard her grandmother swear. But perhaps she was right: Jas was a fool, bloody or otherwise. A fool who was hurting her and didn't seem to care. And she'd begun to laugh at how stupid it all was, how ridiculous: the swearword, Jas's foolishness, and her own.

There was a small crowd outside the cinema. Couples, families with older kids, a few groups of about Chloe's age; Chloe recognised Alice among them, who'd worked a few morning shifts with her at the café, asked if Chloe wanted to earn some cash waitressing at her boyfriend's parents' Christmas party. That must be him there – good-looking, in a clean-cut way, though not a patch on Jas (who was?). He and Alice were standing close together in matching black puffer jackets, Alice's head leaning on his shoulder; she saw Chloe and waved, and Chloe waved back, swallowing the lump in her throat. 'Come on, Grandma,' she said. 'Let's get in line.'

A large woman was moving up and down the queue carrying a tray of paper cups: early sixties, Chloe guessed, one of those beaming volunteer types (there'd been many on the PTA at Chloe's school), the white bobble of her Santa hat bouncing on her shoulder as she approached. 'Happy Christmas,' she said. She was all dressed in red, round and jaunty as a robin perched on a branch. 'Welcome to Lenbourne Community Cinema.

house.'

Small clouds of steam rose from the cups, trailing the scent of cloves and stewed tannins. 'There's mulled apple juice, too.'

Chloe shook her head. 'I'm eighteen,' she said, taking two cups, passing one to Irene. 'I just look really young.'

'You *are* really young, Chloe.' Irene took her cup, stared down into it. 'Is that all we're getting?'

Santa-Hat laughed. 'There's top-ups inside. Three pounds a glass. And mince pies. One pound fifty.' Then, looking down at Irene's stick, she said, 'Why don't I help you to your seat? Can't have you standing around out here in the cold.'

'VIP treatment,' Irene said as they settled in their row. 'I could get used to this.'

'So you should.'

Chloe bundled her coat under her chair. She'd finished her thimbleful of wine, and already her cheeks were warm: she wasn't used to drinking wine, still disliked it really, though the mulled wine was good, better than the rich, dark French stuff her dad bought, which tasted like blackberries and stained her lips. When they were thirteen, she and Lina had spent a Saturday evening working their way through a trio of bottles from Lina's parents' rack: a white, a red and a rosé, followed by way too much tequila. They'd been sick, both of them, one after the other, and woken feeling so rough they'd vowed never to drink again. Her mother had way overreacted – Chloe had been grounded for a fortnight, twice as long as Lina – but Grandma Irene had said only, 'Go easier next time. It's not a race to the bottom of the bottle. The good stuff should be savoured.' Irene was cool like that – nothing seemed to shock her. Perhaps that was why Chloe had ended up telling her, and only her, about Jas.

'What have you dragged me here to see again?' Irene said now. 'I can't remember.'

Chloe turned to look at her. '*Love Actually*, Grandma. I haven't dragged you, have I? Are you feeling OK? Is it too much?'

Irene's hot-pink lips twitched into a smile. She hadn't taken off her coat ('bit chilly in here, isn't it, darling?'); it wasn't the fur one, but another of camel-coloured wool with a white sheepskin collar. The wooden handle of her stick – mahogany, shaped like a duck's head, bought for her by Chloe's dad when she'd come out of hospital – was still in one hand. In the other she held her empty paper cup.

'Just joking, Chloe. I'm not totally gaga yet. I've seen it before. There's a precocious little boy, in love with a little American girl, and Liam Neeson, sad because his wife has died, and Emma Thompson standing looking dignified and heartbroken in her bedroom because Alan Rickman has been cheating on her with some hot young thing from the office. As husbands tend to do. Now' – she handed the cup to Chloe – 'if you could just get me a top-up before the film starts, you'll be making an old woman very happy.'

Chloe rose to her feet. 'Not so old, Grandma.'

Irene was reaching into her purse. 'Chloe, I'm ninety-two. I nearly died last year. Let's not pretend.' She handed Chloe a ten-pound note. 'Get yourself an apple juice, too. Can't have you stumbling back to your dad's blind drunk.'

'Dad wouldn't even notice – not tonight. He's on a *date*. Maddy, that woman who runs the bookshop, is coming round for dinner.'

'Is she, indeed? Well. Good for them.'

Chloe checked her mobile in the queue for the bar – a trestle table, really, manned by Santa-Hat and a man in a matching outfit who might have been her husband, or her twin. Jas. *OK. I can borrow Mum's car. Driving down tomorrow. Tell me where to meet you. J. PS Chloe – please remember, this is just as friends. It has to be, right?*

Just as friends. For God's sake. He'd been texting her all the time since he'd got back from Glasgow. Back and forth all day, and half the night. It was the main reason she'd decided to go back to London for Christmas – well that, and the fact she just couldn't face spending Christmas Day in that horrible house with her dad. Too depressing for words. More guilt – she didn't want to leave her dad by himself, but she felt bad about not being with her mum, too, and Jas was in London, and she'd thought . . . Well, it was obvious what she'd thought. And it had seemed obvious that it was what Jas had been thinking, too.

Make up your mind, Jas, Chloe wrote back, her forefinger and thumb moving furiously over the screen. *I've got enough fucking friends.* And then, just as she reached the front of the queue and Santa-Hat's broad, over-bitten smile, Chloe deleted the message and wrote instead, *OK. Great. Park on Market Square. I'll come and find you.*

Chloe had never spent Christmas in Lenbourne. Christmas, until very recently, had meant either a week in Poole with Grandma Hazel and Grandpa Bill, or either set of grandparents – not that Irene, alone as she was, really constituted a set – coming to stay with them in London. Occasionally, all three had come – Hazel, Bill and Irene in their cracker hats, forming an uneasy trio across one side of the big oak dining table.

'Never again, Peter,' she'd heard her mum say to her dad

in the hallway after one of these Christmases, once the last of the grandparents had left (Irene, puttering off back to Kent in her ancient rust bucket of a car, its white-leather seats stained yellow with age and nicotine).

Her dad had shrugged, run a hand through what was left of his hair. 'I thought it went all right.'

'That's because *you* didn't notice your mother flirting with Bill the whole time.'

'Flirting? Mum doesn't flirt. For God's sake, Laura, she's eighty-eight.'

'So what? Didn't you see her, fluttering her eyelashes at him, touching his arm, laughing at all his jokes? She hardly speaks to Mum, but she hangs off Bill's every word.'

'She's just being friendly.'

Her mum had coughed, disbelieving. 'You're blind, Peter, you really are. Blind and clueless. *That* is the problem.'

Chloe had known about her parents' problems for a while. They'd tried to hide it from her, but not very successfully: that time, for instance, they hadn't known she was watching, that the dining-room door was ajar. The year she turned twelve, her dad had moved into the guest room; they said it was because he snored, but Chloe knew, even then, that this wasn't the whole truth. It wasn't that big a deal: the majority of the parents of Chloe's friends were divorced or separated. Lina's parents, and her own, were the exception.

And yet, when they had finally announced that they were splitting, that her father was moving out, Chloe had been angry with her mother: furious, really, in a way she couldn't quite make sense of, even to herself. Laura swore there had been no affair, and Chloe believed her, even through her fury – and yet she'd blamed her mother all the same. She'd withdrawn from her, turned away – as much as anyone could, shut up in the

44

house together like prisoners during the endless lockdowns. Instead, she'd turned to Lina, to Jas; to her dad, to Irene.

There, too, her grandmother had surprised her. They'd been speaking on FaceTime: this was before Irene's illness and the vaccines, before Chloe's move to Lenbourne with Dad, in the time when the world had been stilled, holding its breath. Chloe had suggested they buy Irene an iPad for Christmas, which she'd had to spend alone in the house on Nelson Street, drinking vermouth and eating artichoke hearts from the jar (or so she had described it to Chloe).

Irene couldn't quite get the hang of the iPad: she never held the screen in the right position to allow a clear view of her face. In this moment, then, Chloe had been telling her grandmother's chin how much her mother annoyed her, how cold and selfish she was, how she was refusing to give her dad a chance to put things right.

'Chloe, darling,' Irene had said, 'I think your mother's given your dad quite enough chances, don't you? They both have. When a marriage isn't working, it just isn't working. There isn't always anyone to blame.'

The chin was still. Chloe, curled on her bed, stared at the section of green-striped wallpaper that, along with the gold-embossed corner of a picture frame, was all she could see of her grandmother's living room. The frame, she knew, contained a watercolour print of Lake Windermere, where Irene and her ex-husband had gone on honeymoon – Chloe's grandfather, of course, though Chloe didn't think of him as such: she had never met him, he'd moved away to Australia after the divorce. Nobody ever talked about him, not Irene, not her dad, not her uncle Richard. No one. All she knew she had learnt by listening in corners, long after she should have been in bed.

'There was in your case, though, wasn't there, Grandma?

45

It was Grandpa Ken's fault you got divorced, not yours. Because of what he did to you. How he was.'

Grandpa Ken: the words sounded strange on her lips. Unfamiliar.

Chloe held her breath, wondering if she'd gone too far. Her grandmother's chin didn't move. Then the screen did, juddering and shaking, bringing Irene's face into view: a face that was staring back at her, the screen tilted upwards, the angles odd, foreshortened.

'Perhaps,' she said. She wasn't smiling, but she wasn't frowning, either. 'But even that wasn't as simple as you think. Nothing ever is.'

On Sunday morning, she went to visit Irene, walking the short distance from her father's rented house to her grandmother's flat. The sun was out, wintry and slanting; the town was sparkling, washed-clean, slow and sleepy in the pale rising light.

Chloe drew her phone from her pocket, took a couple of photographs: a row of wood-framed houses on Church Street, low and huddled, looking as if they might collapse at any moment; the town hall on Market Square, with its clock and its colonnades. There was a Christmas tree outside it, thirty feet high, its coloured lights shattering the sun. Gifts were stacked at the bottom: empty boxes, Chloe presumed, wrapped in foil. She took a photo and sent it to Lina, adding, *Wouldn't get away with this in London, would you? They'd all have been nicked by now.*

The café was already open: Harvey was behind the counter in his apron, filling the hopper with fresh beans. She stepped in,

46

and he turned and said, smiling through his beard, 'Can't keep away, Chloe? You're not in till tomorrow, are you?'

She shook her head. He had Spotify on the speakers as usual: more of that depressing American acoustic stuff he liked. A version of 'Driving Home for Christmas' sung by a guy who sounded like he was about to crash his car into a tree. 'My dad drinks cafetière stuff. Too gross. Can you do me two flat whites to go?'

'Course I can, girl.' They all said that around here; it was one of the first things she'd noticed since coming out to Kent. She liked it; it made her smile.

Her grandmother answered the door in her dressing gown and pyjamas: old flannel ones, Chloe noted with satisfaction. 'Chloe darling.' Irene moved forward to kiss her on both cheeks, trailing her usual scent: Chanel No. 5 and a faint, almost undetectable ammoniac tang (Irene wore incontinence pads now, a fact Chloe had never dared to acknowledge aloud).

'You're early. Alina's still here. I've had my bath. We were just having a quick cup of tea.'

'Oh. I brought you this.' Chloe handed her grandmother a coffee, and Irene beamed and said, 'How lovely of you, darling. I'd just finished my tea anyway.'

Alina appeared behind her in the hallway: a small, slender woman with short black hair, buttoning her coat on over her tunic. Pretty: something of Kristen Stewart about her, when she'd had that dark crop. 'It's all right, Irene. I'm just going.'

Chloe stepped into the hall, leaving the door open. 'Hi, Alina.'

Alina shot her a quick smile and darted out on to the landing. 'Hi, Chloe. Happy Christmas. I'll see you tomorrow morning, Irene.'

In the bedroom, her grandmother's outfit was already laid out on the bed: a yellow jumper, navy skirt, nude-coloured tights and slip. Chloe helped her to dress, averting her eyes from the sight of her grandmother in her bra and pants: not for herself – she loved her, every inch of her – but for Irene. Then she made the bed, tugging the duvet straight, arranging the cushions, collecting the book Irene was reading – A Mistletoe Murder by P.D. James – from where it lay on the carpet, its spine splayed. Irene sat on the blue-linen armchair in the window, watching.

'You spoke to Dad,' Chloe said, placing the last of the cushions on the bed.

'I didn't tell him anything specific, Chloe. I just said that you weren't doing so well, and that he should try talking to you.'

Chloe straightened the cushions, ran a smoothing hand across the duvet. Standing, she said, 'I get it. I know you were worried about me.'

'I was, Chloe. I was. How are you? Was it terrible, seeing him?'

Jas, drawing up on Market Square in his mum's Range Rover. Stepping out, taking measure of the place. Chloe had arrived early, had watched him from under the concealing shadows of the colonnades. He looked different: he'd had his hair cut shorter, his jacket was new. There was something incongruous about seeing him standing there in Lenbourne, looking around him with a perceptible curl of the lip. He hated provincial towns, and not only because he assumed – wrongly, Chloe knew – that everyone in them was at worst racist, at best small-minded. He liked to be near the centre of things, the pulse and thrust. 'I could never live outside a big city,' he'd said to her once, 'could you?' And she'd felt the small cruelty of this question, among all the other, larger cruelties: the knowledge he must surely have had that in asking her to picture her future, he was necessarily asking her to imagine a life without him.

'Yes,' Chloe said.

Irene gave a nod, rose to her feet. She'd left her stick in the hallway – Chloe moved over to her, took her by the arm. Irene leant forward, placed a hand to her chin, let go.

For Alina

It had all begun with her falling down the stairs.

A Thursday afternoon in February, dull and heavy-skied. Irene had been at home for what had felt like forever: months, years, decades. The pandemic had played havoc with time: she didn't even wear her watch any more, and when the batteries in the kitchen clock had failed she hadn't bothered to replace them.

Irene had never much minded solitude – she'd chosen it over marriage, after all, though that had not felt like so much of a choice at the time – but this had been different. She'd spent Christmas alone (Peter and Chloe had got her an iPad, but she loathed the thing). The closest she'd come to any of her family in months had been to stand on the doorstep waving while they shouted at her from the garden gate. An absurd carry-on, necessary though everyone insisted it was; death didn't faze her, not really, not when she was already so close. But she'd had the vaccines by then – there were some perks, at least, to being ancient. Just a couple more weeks and she'd be able to see them all again. Peter and Chloe (Laura, too, perhaps, though the divorce naturally made things difficult); Richard and Katie and the boys.

All the more ironic that it had happened then, when Irene

had been almost at the finish line. Three o'clock, or there-abouts; she'd been sitting in her armchair in the living room, dozing a little after lunch. The radio on: she'd woken to Chopin – one of the Preludes – and sat there for a while in the murky semi-darkness, unable to muster the energy even to get up and turn on a lamp. There had seemed no point to it; suddenly, there had seemed no point to anything. Irene might have closed her eyes and drifted back to sleep, and never woken again: this had seemed preferable, in that moment, to lifting herself painfully from her chair. Then Chopin had given way to Bach, whom Irene loved above all – the Goldberg Variations, played by Glenn Gould – and this had roused her, shaken her out of her stupor. This was no good at all; she'd better get up, turn on a light, find something to do. Her book was in the bed-room; she'd go and find it, make a cup of tea, sit here and read. Anything to flush away the darkness of another lonely winter afternoon.

Irene had gone upstairs, found the book – and it was then, on the landing, that it had happened. Well, two things had. The first was that she'd seen Ken: clear as anything, unmistakable, the bulk of him, standing outlined in the doorway of what had once been the boys' room.

For a moment she'd done nothing – just stared at him, not daring even to breathe. He'd stared back. Said nothing. Not moved an inch. His eyes were on her, though: she felt them, the cruelty in them, the dislike. And so she'd moved, turned and fled, landing awkwardly on the second stair. Her ankle gave way, and she fell.

She'd come to in the ambulance, staring into the kind blue eyes of a paramedic. No pain yet – they must have given her something – but she could tell that there was something wrong with her leg. The paramedic asked what had happened, and

Irene told her that she'd lost her footing; it was a dull, dark day and she hadn't bothered to turn on the light. Lucky, the woman said, that she'd been wearing her alert button, otherwise who knew what might have happened? That blasted thing: her sons had got it for her, mostly she forgot to wear it. Yes, Irene agreed, she'd been lucky. She said nothing about Ken.

Irene had rationalised the moment away. She couldn't have seen him – he was in Australia, wasn't he, had been for years. And anyway, the Ken she'd seen was not the age he would be now – ninety-five, or would it be ninety-six? He'd been younger, standing there, staring at her – fifty or so. The age he'd been when he'd left.

Clearly, she was losing her mind: this was the end. But it hadn't been – she'd only broken her leg; it was a bad fracture, painful, but it would heal. She might have been home again in a couple of weeks if it hadn't been for the chest infection. And then that had turned into pneumonia and she really had nearly died; and Irene did wonder, sometimes, if it might have been better if she had.

Nothing was the same now: she was weak, pathetically so, couldn't even get herself in and out of the bath, and her leg hadn't fused properly. There was a lot of pain, managed with a kitbag of drugs, and her independence and dignity had been dispensed with overnight. Nurses to wash her and feed her and wipe her bottom; doctors to issue the pills and godlike pronouncements on her progress. Her sons taking charge, talking about a 'home' (that euphemism – there was surely nothing remotely homelike about such a place). For God's sake, no. She'd put up a fight about that, the fight of her life, and won the battle, if not the war.

Nelson Street sold. This flat, God's waiting room. The carers who came and went each day, washing and wiping and bringing

53

microwaveable meals Irene mostly threw in the bin uneaten: she didn't have much of an appetite, never had. At least she could still get out and about a bit, with her stick and her trolley, even if it took her an age just to get to the end of the close. At least Peter was close by now, and Chloe, too, for a while. At least she hadn't, yet, seen Ken again.

'How is the temperature, Irene?'

'Good. It's good.' Irene lowered herself gently into the bath, gripping the handrail. Immersed, she leant back, closed her eyes; the temperature really was good, perfect in fact, and Alina had filled the tub right up, even added a slick of the rose bubble bath Katie and Richard had got her for her birthday. None of the other carers took such trouble: her bath, with them, was an inch or two of tepid water, the briefest of soakings. A rough towel-dry, and off they went, with barely a goodbye.

Alina was different. Irene had known it from the first moment she'd arrived, five months ago now: small, rather elegant – 'gamine' was the word that had sprung to Irene's mind, with her cropped dark hair and dainty features, like those actresses from 1960s French films, the ones who'd worn striped tops and had complicated love affairs.

Her English was lightly accented, precise. 'Hello, Mrs Newton. My name is Alina Florescu. I am here to take care of you.'

Irene had felt self-conscious undressing that first time, as she always did before strangers, aware of the ugliness of her body, its puckers and tucks, the long seam just below her knicker-line (Peter had been born by Caesarean) and the other, secret scars. None of the legions of people who had seen her naked in the months since her fall – the nurses, the doctors, the other carers –

had said anything about these, but Alina, gently helping her to remove her pyjama top, had traced the longest one, across her upper back, with her hand, and said, 'A man did this to you. Yes?'

Irene had flinched, and Alina, colouring, had drawn the towel around Irene's chest, knotted it, then laid the pyjama top carefully on the bed. 'I am very sorry, Mrs Newton. I should not have touched you. I should not have said this.'

'It's all right.' It was. 'Yes. A man did do that. But it was a very long time ago.'

That first day, once Irene was washed and dressed, Alina had offered to make her a cup of tea; and then, at Irene's insistence, she had made one for herself too and stayed to drink it, the two of them sitting in the kitchen at the pine table, the radio that had become Irene's constant companion turned down low. 'Bartók,' Alina had said, and Irene had smiled and said, 'Yes. You like classical music?'

Alina had shrugged, looked away. 'I did. I do.'

Irene didn't know how Alina managed it; the others were never there for longer than fifteen minutes, but that first time, and every other time since (Alina came five mornings a week), she had stayed for an hour. Presumably she was late for her other appointments: she had admitted, a few weeks later, that her supervisors were angry with her, that she had been disciplined for taking too long. Alina's dark eyes had narrowed, then: there was a fierceness there, one Irene respected, understood. 'It's ridiculous. You cannot care for someone, not properly, in fifteen minutes.'

'No,' Irene had said. 'It's true. You can't.'

Now, months later, they had slipped into an easy routine: undressing, bathing, drying, dressing again. Alina helped Irene to dry her hair, apply her make-up: she wasn't as steady with her lipstick as she had once been. Then she made them both tea, and they sat and drank it, and they talked: about not very much at first – the weather, the news, how and where Alina had learnt English – and then, gradually, about the things that mattered. The medical degree Alina had been halfway through when she'd left Bucharest and could not now afford to take up again. Her two boys, Mihai and Gabriel, who were seven and five; her sister Daniela, who was married to a local man. 'Eddy,' she said. 'He's a mechanic. A good man.' Irene, listening, had understood that there was another man Alina was referring to, in the spaces between her words – one who was not so good. But she had not enquired further; she would not pry.

There had been something about Alina that had seemed familiar to Irene. She had puzzled over this; wondered, for a long while, if they might somehow have met before, or seen each other around town. It was possible: Alina had been in Lenbourne for three years now. Her brother-in-law, Eddy, owned Valley Motors, where Irene had her car serviced. Daniela did the books, so Irene might have seen Alina there, dropping in on her sister, but this seemed unlikely; perhaps it had been Daniela whom Irene had noticed, though Alina swore that they didn't look at all alike. Daniela was tall, blonde, well built, 'a Viking,' Alina said, 'not like the rest of us at all. My father used to joke that my mother must have had a secret lover. A man from Sweden.'

And then, gradually, Irene had realised what it was, this familiarity: a sense of recognition that was not literal, that somehow transcended words. She'd felt it before, with a couple of friends, and with strangers, even: a woman at the checkout in Tesco, the lady in the post office who could never quite meet her eye. A kinship; an instinctive understanding that they were living as she once had, that they knew what she knew, and that they carried the weight of this knowledge with them, through each night, each day. The knowledge that the man they lived with hated them, though he might call it love. The knowledge that they were not safe and might never feel so again, not truly; even if the man was gone, even if he had been on the other side of the world for forty years.

Peter had suggested that Irene buy her Christmas presents online this year: she had the iPad, and Chloe had set her up with an Amazon account and something called PayPal.

The internet really was a remarkable invention – Irene had ordered a CD of Bach cantatas one afternoon, and it had arrived the next day – but there was something about the ease of online shopping that unsettled her. It was almost *too* convenient, she felt. No shop, surely, online or otherwise, could supply *everything*, and not be cutting corners somewhere along the line. And anyway, if everyone bought everything they needed there, then what would happen to towns like Lenbourne? All the shops would close – too many of them already had – and we'd be back to where we were in the 1970s. Irene remembered it clearly: the empty storefronts, the derelict dance halls and cinemas, everyone driving off to the out-of-town supermarkets and shopping centres, thinking they were cruising towards a better, brighter future.

'If we're not careful,' she'd told Peter, 'we'll end up like America. Cars everywhere. No pavements. Nowhere to walk.'

Peter had eyed her cautiously. They did that these days, all of them: looked at her as if she were made of china, as if she might be about to break. All of them except Chloe and Alina.

'It's not like that everywhere in America, Mum,' he said. 'And anyway, how would you know? You've never been.'

'I wanted to go. Still would, given half a chance. Boston. New York. The Chicago Symphony.'

He'd smiled. He was looking tired, her younger son: tired and sad and worn out. What was he now: fifty-five, fifty-six? In her mind he was still five, that quiet, watchful boy, with his wooden train set and the stuffed rabbit he'd carried with him everywhere, greying and threadbare – for comfort, of course. He'd seen too much, they both had, her boys, though she'd done her best to shield them.

'Maybe one day, Mum,' he'd said.

Irene had allowed the lie to stand. Anyway, Peter was right: it would be too much for her to get round the shops this year. She'd give everybody money for Christmas; there wasn't much left since Nelson Street had been sold, the flat paid for, the carers and alarm systems and all the rest of it, but there was something. She'd still get a few small gifts – things she could wrap – for Chloe and the boys. And for Alina. Yes, she would get something for Alina, too.

Irene ventured out on a fine afternoon, frosty and crisp. She wore the mink – it didn't get out much these days either, and hang anyone who disapproved; that wasn't going to bring the poor creatures back to life, was it? – and a hat she'd bought herself a decade or so ago which Chloe said made her look Russian. 'A glamorous Russian, Gran,' she'd added, and Irene had thought of Lara in *Dr Zhivago*: Julie Christie, blonde and smouldering under grey rabbit fur. Perhaps there had once been a resemblance.

'A babushka, more like,' she'd said to Chloe; but still, the compliment had pleased her. Irene always had been too susceptible to flattery: it was, she'd decided (she'd had a great deal of time, over the years, to consider this, to weigh one defect against another, and each virtue too), her fatal flaw.

'You're exquisite,' Ken had said to her the first time they met: a Friday evening at the Odeon in Canterbury, full skirts and shirt-waisters, a big band, still a few years to go before the arrival of rock'n'roll. Irene was twenty-two, blonde and slender, a dead ringer for Grace Kelly, everyone said so, and almost as elegant, though her dad was a bus driver, her mum a housewife and they lived in a bungalow in Wincheap. She was an apprentice seam-stress in a city-centre boutique, tailoring affordable replicas of the latest fashions from Paris and America; Irene cut the patterns, was learning to sew seams and sleeves, and modelled prototypes for the customers. She'd been as stupid and empty-headed, it seemed to Irene now, as it had been possible for a girl to be; she'd had boyfriends, queues of them, but not one of them as tall and broad and definite as Ken Newton. A man, not a boy; she'd felt tiny in his arms, and he'd had to bend almost in two to whisper in her ear. 'Exquisite'; nobody had called her this before. Oh, Ken had known how to work her, right from the moment they'd met.

It was a short walk from the flat to Market Square. Irene took her time, leaning on her trolley, her stick inside it, just for back-up. Passed a few people she knew – Margaret Curran, who'd worked with Ken at Williams and Jenkins, years ago; Ron Armstrong, who was a lay preacher at St Michael's these days. Ron stopped, asked her how she was doing, said he'd heard she'd moved into sheltered accommodation. He was a kind man, always had been; a few years her junior, and not unattractive. There might have been something between them once, but he was married, of course; they'd all been married, by the time she wasn't any more.

'Haven't seen you at church for a while,' Ron said. 'Will you be coming to midnight Mass?'

'Perhaps. It's not so easy these days, you know . . .'

He smiled. 'Of course. Well, Irene, it's good to see you looking so well.'

Did she? Was he just sparing her the truth? She caught a glimpse of herself in the window of the butcher's: an old lady, pushing a shopping trolley, swathed absurdly in layers of fur, wearing a hat that was frankly ridiculous. She stopped, deflated; stood and stared at the trays of glistening flesh, the plump chicken breasts and rib-eyes and strings of sausages. The queue was spilling out on to the pavement; the butchers, in their white coats, were busy, dispensing bacon and pigs in blankets, hams and stuffing, and turkeys in cardboard carriers, like pets from the store.

They'd had a kitten once, when the boys were small; Ivy, Ken had called her – he'd brought her back from the pet shop in just such a box, a box with holes in the lid. He'd meant well, Irene supposed, though the name had been too much, too painful: it had been twelve years since they'd lost her – the other Ivy – but it was still as raw as if it had only happened the day before. And the kitten, when she grew into a cat, had got on Ken's nerves. Irene had come home one day with the boys to find that he'd got rid of her, given her away to a friend of his, a drinking buddy who lived on the other side of town. Richard and Peter had been inconsolable. 'Don't see what all the fuss is about,' Ken had said. 'I bought the bloody thing, didn't I? So I get to decide what happens to it.'

Ken. The shape of him, standing there on the landing, blocking out the light.

'Are you all right?' A woman, middle-aged, blonde – smart in her black padded coat, her diamond earrings – was staring at her from the queue.

'I'm quite all right, thank you,' Irene said. But she wasn't:

her leg was hurting, her brain had clouded, she'd forgotten to take her tablets. Irene turned, pushed herself and the trolley away from the blonde woman, from the butcher's shop, from all that nauseating uncooked meat and dived into the nearest open door. Boots. Strip-lighting. Calm. Tinny pop music, a woman not wanting much for Christmas, only you. Which was, surely, the world.

Oh, Irene was tired. So tired. She could lie down right there, on the linoleum floor, and go to sleep. But Alina: she'd wanted to buy something for Alina. Alina, with her kindness, and her sadness, and the silences between her words. Irene reached for the closest shelf – smelly stuff, lotions and potions. Picked one at random, in a box made to look like a Christmas cracker. It would do, wouldn't it? It wasn't much, perhaps, but it would have to do.

That night, Irene saw him for the second time.

She'd woken in the small hours – she didn't sleep well; hadn't for years – and lain for a while, as she often did, her eyes closed, counting her breaths, the rise and fall of her chest, in the way Peter had taught her. *One. Two. Three.* It was no good: her mind was overactive at this time, alert and skittish. And the room was stuffy: the flats were heated from a central boiler, as if residents couldn't be trusted to monitor their own body temperature, and in winter they kept the radiators on all night. She'd get up, open a window, have a drink and a cigarette, maybe read a little. Her insomniac ritual.

It was in the living room, then, that Irene saw him. She was moving slowly round the room, stick in one hand, glass of vermouth in the other, turning on the lamp, the tree. She sensed movement at the limit of her vision – the briefest flash, an animal's quick, darting silhouette – and turned, and Ken was there, standing outlined against the open door. Younger than the last time: in his thirties, his hair still dark and thick. She stared at his shoes – those polished brogues he'd worn to the office every day; they'd bought them together, on a day trip to London, along with a new suit for his new job. An open-top bus ride; ice creams in St James's Park. Perhaps he'd been happy, then – perhaps they both had. Before Ivy. Before.

Finally, she lifted her eyes to his face. He was staring at her again, those black eyes fixed on hers, but his expression was different this time, filled not with dislike but with something softer, more diffuse. Irene blinked, looked again, and saw that he was crying; and she understood it then, knew with a certainty that she couldn't even try to explain – she wouldn't know how to begin to explain it, even to herself – that he was gone, as Ivy was gone, and that, on some level, he was sorry.

'My son Peter brought mince pies,' Irene said. 'Will you have one?'

Alina nodded. She was standing by the kettle in her blue tunic, the mugs, milk and teabags already arranged on the counter. 'I got such a shock, the first time I had Christmas here. Eddy said there was this lovely cake I needed to try, this English tradition. He gave me one, and when I bit into it he told me what it was called – "mince pie". I spat it out at once. I thought it was *mince*, you know – like beef.'

Irene laughed. 'English can be so confusing, can't it?'

'It can.' The kettle clicked; Alina poured water into the mugs. 'Where are they, these pies? I will get them for you.'

'In that cupboard there – the one where the sugar is.' Alina opened the cupboard, drew out the box. 'Oh, and Alina – could you do one other thing for me, if you don't mind?'

'Of course.'

'Go into the living room, please, and have a look under the tree.' Irene shifted her gaze to the table, to the gnarled landscape of her hand, spread out against the wood. 'There's something there for you.'

Alina slipped from the room. She returned carrying her gift in its silver paper, her cheeks pink. 'You did not need to do this, Irene. Really, you did not.'

'I know I didn't. I wanted to.'

'You are very kind.' Alina set the present down on the table, together with the mugs of tea, and two cold mince pies on a plate. Irene would have preferred hers warm, with cream, but she said nothing. Alina's dark head dipped below the table; she was rummaging in her handbag, a huge black plastic-leather thing that Irene suspected weighed a ton. She didn't know how such a small woman could manage, lugging such a thing around all day; it was incredible, really, the things that women carried around.

When Alina raised her head again, she was smiling. 'It is good that I got something for you too, Irene, or I would have felt very bad. Very guilty.'

Alina laid a second gift on the table: this one was small, square, soft-looking – some kind of fabric, perhaps? A tea towel? It was wrapped in shiny red paper, printed with small green holly leaves and tied with gold ribbon. The label – Irene picked up the present, held it in her hand – read, *To Irene, my favourite patient and, I hope, my friend. Love, Alina* X.

'It's only a small thing,' Alina said, and Irene swallowed, laid the gift back down and said, 'Thank you. Really. I think of you as a friend, too.'

'Well, then. We are lucky, I think.'

'Yes. We are.'

They drank their tea, they ate the pies. Irene's was a little dry – perhaps it was longer since Peter had brought them than she'd thought – but Alina ate hers quickly, neatly, holding the foil case below her mouth to catch the crumbs.

The things that Irene had thought about telling Alina sat heavily in her mind. That she'd seen her ex-husband twice, though such a thing was impossible; that she was sure, absolutely sure, that he was dead. Not that she'd seen his ghost, exactly – she wasn't as crazy as all that – but some sort of after-image, some type of transmitted knowledge that was beyond reason, beyond science. Such things happened: her mother had told a story about a friend who'd gone for lunch with her fiancé during wartime, held him in her arms to say goodbye, and received a telegram later that day saying that his plane had been shot down over Dieppe two days before.

Hours she'd spent on the iPad during the night, typing his name into Google: there were plenty of Kenneth Newtons in Australia – an orthodontist in Adelaide; a landscape gardener in Wollongong – but none of them was him, at least as far as she could tell. Even this hadn't made the slightest dent in Irene's certainty; perhaps he'd changed his name. She felt she ought to tell the boys – *men*, of course: they were fifty-six and sixty years old – but she didn't know where to begin. *Your father is dead, I know he is, and I know because I saw him, twice, with my own eyes.* They'd think she'd finally gone round the bend, when she had never felt more lucid about anything in her life.

And the rest of it, too – the other burden she carried, that they both had, she and Ken. Ivy. Their firstborn. The small weight of her, in her arms; Irene had insisted on holding her, though they hadn't wanted her to, the midwives, they'd wanted to wrap her in the sheet and carry her away. Ken hadn't seen her; he'd gone back outside to the corridor as soon as he'd heard the word, its ugliness, its blunt finality. *Stillborn*. When he'd come back in and seen Irene's arms empty – for they had carried Ivy away in the end, they'd had to, she hadn't been able to stop them – he'd seemed different, somehow. Tougher, harder-edged. Perhaps it had always been there, his capacity for cruelty, but it was this that had loosened it, set it free. Ken had blamed her, Irene knew he had; he'd blamed her, as surely as she'd blamed herself.

All this she had thought about telling Alina – offering it to her as she had offered it to no one before, watching her listen, her brown eyes steady, calm. But now the words lodged in her throat; it seemed absurd to her now, in the cool light of a December morning, to speak of such things, to expose all that violence and loss to the air. She drank her tea and said, 'You can open your present, if you like. Or would you rather wait?'

Alina smiled. 'I'll open it, if you'll open yours.'

'All right.'

She watched Alina unwrap her gift; it seemed meagre, a sorry token, just a couple of bottles of smelly stuff swathed in plastic. But Alina seemed to like it; she took out the bottles, opened them, passed them to Irene to smell. 'Delicious,' Alina said, the word rolling around her mouth like a marble. 'It smells of summer. Sunshine in a bottle.'

Irene smiled. 'As long as you like it.'

'Really, I do. Thank you. A treat. Now it's your turn.'

Irene reached for the square packet in its red wrapping, opened it carefully, making sure not to tear the paper. Inside she found an apron: white, with black halter and ties, printed with the image of a black cat, stirring what looked like a mug of tea with its paw. Below it, in bold capitals, were the words *I Do What I Want.*

'It's not much,' Alina said. 'I hope it is not too – what is the word? – *tacky.*'

'No.' Perhaps it was, a little, but no matter. 'I like it. Thank you. Put it on me. Go on – I want to wear it now.'

Alina got up from her chair. Irene stood too, feeling the creak and strain of her muscles, her ligaments, her old bones. Alina slipped the apron over her head, drew the ties together at her waist. Irene turned to face her, and Alina said, 'There. It looks good on you, I think. It's silly, I know, but I like what it says. The message. I think you are very independent, Irene. Very strong.'

'Thank you.' She stood facing Alina, looking at her; Alina met her gaze. Neither woman spoke. After a moment, Irene reached for Alina's hand, held it for one second, two, three. 'It's lovely. It really is.'

For Daniela

Christmas, when they were small, had meant a drive to their grandmother's house in the countryside, close to Snagov; the two of them, Alina and Daniela, huddled together on the back seat, humming along to the Beatles songs their mother played over and over on cassette.

Rubber Soul, Revolver, Abbey Road. Alina would learn the album titles later, and the lyrics – but then, there had been something dreamlike about the music, with its beat and its jangle and their mother singing tunelessly along.

Their mother's name was Alexandra, though everyone called her Lexi, except the girls, who of course knew her as Mama; she was a lecturer in English, or had been until having them. Lexi still taught privately: thin, pinched-looking university students, mainly boys, whom she would meet at the door and show to the small box room at the furthest end of the apartment that she still called her 'study'.

Lexi loved England; she had spent a year in Manchester, one of only a handful of students from their country permitted the honour of continuing their studies in the West. Those twelve months – the high, red-brick buildings, the rain, the clubs she went to with the friends she made there, dancing until morning – formed part of family folklore. Alina and Daniela had heard their mother's stories of England so often that they had begun to merge, in their minds, with the other, wilder tales their grandmother told them, of wolves and boars and children lost in the mountains, and the picture books their mother read to them each night. Perhaps they had also lost their currency for Lexi, too: she had never returned to England, though she'd sometimes threatened to do so when the girls were particularly naughty. Her student permit had lasted a year; barely three weeks after her return to Bucharest she had met the girls' father, Marius – Tata. Three years later, Daniela had been born; and two years after that, Alina.

Their *bunica* – Sofia, their mother's mother – was a widow who lived alone on a smallholding four miles outside Snagov. Too remote, Mama said: she was often snowed in and there were bears in the forests that surrounded the property. But Bunica said she wasn't going anywhere, not until she dropped dead and they could drag her off her land feet-first. And anyway, bears didn't scare her: she'd come face to face with one once, standing on her front path on its hind legs, and had stared it down until it fell on to its four paws and scampered away, meek as a pet dog. 'Rubbish,' Mama said, and perhaps it was; but the girls believed it, they could believe anything of Bunica, who wore men's coats and gumboots and tied a scarf over her hair, which Mama said made her look like the queen of England. Each Christmas Bunica killed a pig to mark their arrival; they ate parts of it, bacon and sausages and stews and fried *pomana porcului*, each day until their return to Bucharest.

Tata was rarely with them on these annual drives with Mama; he would come later, sometimes not until Christmas Eve. That was the night they decorated Bunica's tree; she always had a real one, so tall its tip brushed the living-room ceiling, cut from the forest by the three huge, silent brothers who ran the neighbouring farm. She kept her boxes of decorations in the attic: ancient baubles and battered tin stars and real candles, thin wax tapers. Mama protested that eventually she would burn the place down, with all of them inside. 'Rubbish,' Bunica shot back. They were as strong as each other, she and Mama; but out on the farm, at Christmas and any other time of year, it was always Bunica who got her way.

The year Alina was eight, and Daniela closer to ten, Tata arrived on Christmas Eve with a boy they did not recognise. He was small and dark, like Tata, like all of them bar Daniela, with her waist-length blonde hair. His sly, darting eyes looked around him, taking everything in.

'This is Andrei,' Tata said. 'Your brother.'

The girls stared at him. The boy stared back, unblinking. Mama said nothing. Bunica, standing beside the tree, a tin star still in her hand, lifted her chin. 'Here,' she said, crossing the room, placing a hand on the boy's shoulder, and with her other offering him the star. 'Come and put this on the tree. There's a space here, I think.'

She led this boy, this Andrei, back across the room to the tree. He fastened the star to a branch, and Bunica cupped the back of his neck and said, 'You are very welcome here, Andrei.'

Daniela and Alina still didn't move; their eyes were on their mother, who was also standing very still, her arms clasped to her sides. Tata, not looking at her, clapped his hands and said, 'Right, I'm starving. Andrei is too. Shall we eat? Where's this pig stew of yours, Sofia?'

This was the first time they had ever learnt of their brother's existence. They would learn more, gradually, over time – the girlfriend Tata had had before Mama; the baby he'd known nothing about until the day the woman had turned up at his

69

office with Andrei in tow. He was fourteen. It was, for Alina, for Daniela too, a watershed, separating one chapter of their lives from the next; though this, too, they had only understood slowly, by degrees.

They were driving to Bluewater. Just the two of them, Alina and Daniela; the kids were with Eddy. 'Go,' he'd said that morning. 'Have a girls' day. Enjoy yourselves. Well, as much as you can in that place, two weeks before Christmas.'

They'd been having breakfast: coffee and foil-wrapped croissants, the kids running in and out. Daniela, standing beside Eddy by the counter, had leant over to kiss him. 'Thanks, *iubire*. That would be great.'

Daniela and Eddy were always like that – well, almost always; it wasn't as if they didn't have the odd argument. But even those tended to be minor. The other day, Daniela had gone to pack Darius's football kit, discovered it still lying dirty and stinking in the basket, and called Eddy at work to have a go at him. She'd been really quite a cow about it, in Alina's opinion – she still couldn't believe Eddy did the laundry – and he'd come home with a bunch of flowers. Eddy put up with too much from Daniela, Alina thought, though of course she kept this to herself. She couldn't remember Dragos ever coming home with flowers for her, even when he'd actually done something worth apologising for.

'Where do you want to start? John Lewis, or Sparky Mark's?'

Alina smiled. This was an old family joke, their mother's word for Marks & Spencer, acquired during her year in Manchester – though Daniela said she had found no one, through all her years in England, who'd ever heard the term, much less used it themselves. 'John Lewis, maybe. Mihai needs a new bag for school. But he says he wants some kind of light for his room. One that projects the planets on to the ceiling.'

His room: a slip of the tongue, a misstep. Mihai shared with his brother and his cousins, now; Eddy and Daniela had bought bunk beds, another set to match the ones they'd already had. Poor Angelica, sharing with three boys. She'd be ten next year: it couldn't continue. None of it could.

But Daniela didn't seem to notice. 'Sounds great. They'll all love it. There's that shop, isn't there – sells science things. Gadgets. We can try in there. And then lunch in that Lebanese place, maybe? If we get the stew we can close our eyes and pretend we're back with Bunica. Minus the pig.'

'Good plan, *sora mea.*'

It felt good, speaking Romanian with Daniela, like putting on an old pair of comfortable shoes. At home, Daniela spoke only English to Eddy and the kids. Eddy had learnt a few words, enough to say 'hello', 'goodbye' and 'thank you' to Mama and Tata on what had once been their annual trip to Bucharest – it was years now since Daniela and her family had returned to Romania – and Angelica and Darius knew only a phrase or two more. Daniela hadn't wanted to bring them up bilingual. 'What possible use could they have for Romanian?' she said. 'It's a dead language, a dead country. My kids are English, through and through.'

It was a shame, Alina thought – a missed opportunity. Though of course now she was trying to reverse the situation, immerse Mihai and Gabriel in English. They were becoming pretty fluent – school helped, of course – but just the other day, Gabriel had come up to her and put his arms around her, in that way he did, sticky fingers and sweet sugar breath (Daniela let them all have too many sweets) and whispered in her ear in

Romanian. *Mamă, can we go to the playground so we can talk? My brain is hurting with all these English words.*

'Hey,' Daniela said now, pressing the accelerator and veering wildly out into the right-hand lane. She wasn't indicating; her sister drove as she lived: boldly. Alina had always been the timid one, the one walking a few steps behind. Andrei had known this; he would never have tried the same things with Daniela. Or perhaps he would; who knew, really, what he was capable of?

'Why,' Daniela said, speeding dangerously close to the car in front, 'is this stupid man driving like an old woman?'

Alina had no answer. She watched the road, the white lines, the blur of trees and houses and scrubby, fractured fields. The countryside was receding now, swallowed by housing estates and warehouses; they were almost there. She breathed deeply, feeling her lungs swell and release, as she had learnt to do in Daniela's yoga class: twenty women lying on their backs in their leggings in the church hall. Alina had been sceptical at first – not least because it cost ten pounds a session, more than she earned in an hour – but it helped. Daniela had said it would, and she'd been right, as she almost always was.

Alina had moved back to their parents' apartment on a bitter November night. Not alone, of course – she'd taken the boys, wrapped them in blankets in the car, both in their pyjamas, sucking their thumbs, their eyes wide and confused as she strapped them into their seats.

Dragos hadn't tried to stop her. They'd known it was coming, she'd had their bags packed for weeks. She hadn't been sure what she was waiting for, really – somebody to give her permission, perhaps, to tell her it was the right thing to do. And that person, as always, had been Daniela. Alina had spoken to her that afternoon on Skype while Dragos was in their bedroom, playing his computer game, the one that occupied every minute of his waking hours, that seemed to matter to him more than anything: more than earning a living, more than Alina, more than his own sons.

'Just go,' Daniela had said, standing tall and blonde and wholesome in her English kitchen, a Viking, all those miles away, with the husband who loved her and bought her flowers and didn't spend almost every moment of every day blowing pixelated soldiers to bits. 'Put the boys in the car and go to Mama and Tata's.'

The words still made Alina wince. 'But Andrei's there.'

Daniela lifted her mug; she was drinking tea, she'd said, real English tea, with milk, not lemon. The mug was white, with the words *World's Greatest Mum* written across it in glittery pink letters. A gift the previous Christmas, Alina knew, from Angelica, who was six now: a lovely child, with her mother's eyes and her father's hair, tugged into tight cornrows. 'I know. But it won't be for long, will it? Just till the apartment's sold. And there's room enough for all of you.'

'Yes, but I . . .'

'Alina. *Soră mai mică.* My little sister. Just go.'

And so Alina had gone, travelling the short distance from the rental she shared with Dragos to the apartment in which she had grown up. The buildings shrank lower as she approached their old street; in the place of all those ugly, faceless blocks here there were still balconies, old-fashioned street lamps, winter pansies planted around the trunks of leafless planes. Tata and Mama had helped plant them; it had been a regular event, four times a year, stepping out with their neighbours on

73

a Sunday morning, carrying trowels and flasks of coffee. Last time, Alina and the boys had joined them; she sat for a moment after parking the car, remembering, feeling the weight of their loss.

The boys were sleeping in the back, breathing heavily through open mouths. A tap came on the window; there, peering in, was Andrei, his face pale and luminous under the street light. He still had the beard he'd had at the funeral. Thick and black, framing wet pink lips.

'Hello, *soră*,' he said. 'Take the boys inside. I'll get the bags.'

Neither Alina nor Daniela could quite work out how Andrei had come to take up residence in their parents' apartment. He hadn't asked either of them whether they minded – but then, they'd reasoned, he didn't have to, not really: the apartment was his as well, the will had divided everything in three. 'Still,' Daniela had said to Alina many times, 'it's weird, if you ask me. Especially when we're selling the place. I mean, it was never *his* home, was it? Doesn't he have anywhere else to go?'

Alina didn't know. Neither of them did. Their half-brother was a mystery to them still: a satellite, moving in and out of their orbit. Semi-delinquent as a teenager – drugs had been involved, they suspected, though nobody had told them so directly. There'd been a spell at a tough school outside Piteşti, paid for by their father (this they knew from the late-night arguments between Tata and Mama). Through his twenties – their own teenage years, then Daniela's accountancy degree and Alina's decision to study medicine – they'd hardly seen Andrei. A couple of Christmases at Bunica's; Tata's sixtieth birthday, celebrated at a beer-house in Lipscani; each time Andrei had seemed restless, unsettled, unable to sit still. There was something about him, something neither of them could quite put her finger on. 'He gives me the creeps,' Daniela said, and Alina agreed. It was the way he looked at you, the way he hardly blinked. Like a lizard. Like something cold and calculating.

Strange things had happened when they were children, things they had not forgotten. That first Christmas, at Bunica's, Daniela had found a dead rat in her bed, right at the bottom, under the tightly tucked sheets; she'd touched it with her bare foot and screamed. 'Poor thing,' Bunica had said, lifting the rat out by its tail. 'It must have crawled in to find somewhere warm to die.' But Daniela and Alina knew this was not what had happened; they knew it, and they suspected that Bunica had known it, too.

That night years later, then – the night Alina had left Dragos – she'd put the boys to bed in the room that had once been theirs, hers and Daniela's. And then Andrei had asked if she would like a cup of coffee.

'Something stronger, I think,' she said. She still couldn't believe she'd really done it, really left. She put a hand to her throat. 'Tata always kept a bottle of *tuica* on top of the fridge.'

Andrei shook his head. They were in the hallway; he was standing between her and the kitchen. She had the oddest feeling that he was blocking her way. 'It's gone. All of it. I threw it all away. I don't drink, Alina, and neither should you. Disgusting stuff. And you're a mother. You should know better.'

She stared at him. He stared back. A tightening in her chest. An instinct. *Run.* But she couldn't, of course – where would she go? And anyway, plenty of people didn't drink; it wasn't so unusual. Who cared if he'd thrown away Tata's ancient supply?

'I'll go to the corner store, then,' she said. 'You can watch the boys for a minute, can't you? They're sleeping again now. Where's the spare key? I couldn't see it on the hook.'

A silence. Tense, for some reason, uncomfortable. Alina told herself she was imagining it: she was tired, so tired, and

75

what possible reason could he have for resisting her wish to go out and buy wine? And yet the silence stretched on; she began to think that Andrei was not going to answer her, not going to give her the key. And then, just as her heart was starting to thud violently in her chest, Andrei reached into his pocket and handed it to her. Mama's old key ring, a pewter model of Big Ben.

'There you go,' he said. 'Take care on the street, Alina, won't you? It's not safe around here. Not at this time of night. Not for a woman alone.'

Outside, she Skyped Daniela; it was two hours earlier in England, her niece and nephew would only just be going to bed. There was her sister, in the bathroom with Darius, his wet hair spiked with shampoo, everything clean and calm and ordinary. 'It's done,' Alina said, 'I've left him.' And in all the fuss that followed – Daniela's whoops and shouts, Angelica coming in, the kids demanding to know what their mum was saying to Tanti Alina – she forgot to say anything to Daniela about Andrei, about that strange scene in the hallway; about the fact that, for a moment, maybe two, she'd been almost afraid of him and of what he might do.

They parted ways outside the restaurant; Alina wanted an hour or so alone.

'Just a few bits I need to get,' she'd said as they finished lunch. Daniela had smiled and drained her glass of sparkling wine: guessing, perhaps, that those 'bits' were for Daniela herself.

Alina's own gift from her sister was, she knew, carefully stored at the bottom of Daniela and Eddy's wardrobe; Daniela was always organised, had started her Christmas shopping the previous January, in the sales. But then it was easy to be organised when you didn't really have to work; or at least, when the work you did – accounting for your husband's garage – fitted into a handful of hours while both your children were at school. It wasn't like spending your time wiping old people's bottoms, was it; but even as Alina thought this, turning away from Daniela, heading back into the milling Christmas crowds, she corrected herself. She loved her job, even if it was not the one she had dreamt of, the one she had studied for. And of all her patients – 'service users', the agency wanted her to call them, but she couldn't think of them that way, as numbers, as bald digits on a graph – she loved Mrs Newton, Irene, most. Her glamour, her spark. She reminded Alina, somehow, of Bunica, though it was impossible to imagine two more different women (nobody could have called her grandmother glamorous). Alina had found a gift for Irene earlier, in one of the cheap seasonal stores that had sprung up around the shopping centre: an apron with a cat on it. Tacky perhaps, but something about it had made Alina think of Irene; and anyway, it had been only £5, and that was the most she could afford to spend.

For Daniela, Alina had reserved almost as much as she was spending on each of the boys: £40, maybe £50 at a pinch. She'd been saving for months, squirrelling away as much as she could. Things were easier while she was staying with Eddy and Daniela – they insisted that she shouldn't pay rent, though as one year had turned into two, and now, horrifyingly, three, Alina had gone ahead and set up a direct debit anyway. She knew it was nowhere near the amount she'd need to pay for her own place, the place she needed to find for herself and the boys, especially now that Eddy and Daniela had put down a deposit on the new development. In the new year, Alina hoped she would have enough saved to cover her own deposit on a new flat, and the first few months' rent. Perhaps she already had enough; perhaps, Alina thought as she moved through the crowds, George Michael crooning from the speakers, what was holding her back from moving out was not a lack of money, but the desire to stay where she was, in her sister's comfortable little house, with her sister there to protect her, to protect them all.

The store Alina wanted was on the first floor, halfway along the parade of more exclusive shops; they rarely came to this side of the centre, she and Daniela, and it was quieter here, almost restful. A wonderful scent hit her as she walked in, something sweet and heady: roses, perhaps, or orange blossom (she was no good with plants). Alina stood for a moment with her eyes closed, breathing in the scent. Perhaps it was the wine they'd had with lunch, but she felt, for a moment, almost dizzy, filled with a sudden inexpressible joy.

'Can I help you?'

Alina opened her eyes; a woman was standing there, slender, heavily made-up, smiling. 'Yes. Sorry. I am here to buy a present for my sister.'

The woman's expression didn't change as Alina spoke; sometimes they did change, English people, when they heard that she was not one of them – though some could tell, she knew, just by looking at her, by observing that she had the wrong hairstyle, or facial features, or cut of jeans. Mama had loved England so much, but perhaps it had been different then; perhaps she had never had anyone turn away from her in a pub, or narrow their eyes at her on the street, or even – one terrible morning Alina tried hard to forget – refuse to let her into their flat because she was a 'dirty bloody gypsy'. She could still picture the old man's face, peering around his front door, contorted into an expression of blind, irrational dislike. Alina had had to leave, call the agency, tell them to send another carer in her place.

'Of course,' the shop assistant said. 'Do you have anything particular in mind?'

Alina did: she'd looked it up online. She drew her phone from her pocket, showed the woman the screenshot she'd saved; the woman nodded, smiled again. She had a lovely smile, Alina decided: she smiled with her eyes as well as her mouth. Not everybody did that. 'Ah yes, we definitely have that in stock. It's just over here.'

The necklace was not large, not showy – how could it be, for the price? – but it was, Alina decided as she held it in her hands, examined it from every angle, just right. A fine chain (gold-plated, but she knew Daniela wouldn't care) holding a small gold bar. 'Have you decided on an inscription?' the shop woman asked, and Alina nodded, took the slip of paper out of her pocket, the paper on which she'd written the words as carefully as she could, each letter broad and clear. *Sora mea, ursoaica.* My sister, the bear.

'Lovely,' the woman said. 'Italian, is it?'

Alina looked at her. 'No. Romanian.'

The shop assistant didn't blink. 'Lovely. Right. Well, we'll get this done for you now. It'll be about half an hour, OK?'

'OK. Thank you. I'll come back then.'

It had been Daniela, again, who had saved her in the end. Saved them all.

Alina had called her from the room, the room that had once been theirs, where the sisters had slept as children, serene and carefree, it seemed to her now, as characters from a storybook set in another place, another time.

The three of them were sharing it by then – Mihai, Gabriel and herself, the two boys in one of the single beds and Alina in the other. Andrei wouldn't let her use her mother's room, the room where Lexi had once taught her students. He said he needed it, said he was using it for prayer. Alina heard him in there, for hours at a time, reciting canticles under his breath. He had found religion, the new orthodoxy, the new way, or so he said; she thought he had gone completely mad. Perhaps he had always been so.

The things he said, the things he had done – Alina hadn't been able to believe it, really, had kept telling herself she was overdramatising, imagining things. When he'd put a lock on the kitchen door, told her that she and the boys were eating too much, that they were greedy pigs, that she would have to ask him for the key every time she or the children wanted something to eat – when he'd done all this, she'd told herself not to worry, that he was just in a mood, that it would pass. But it hadn't passed. It had got worse. Andrei was obsessed with keys, kept them attached to his belt like a jailer. He'd taken away her set, told her she'd have to ring the bell when she went out, and then refused to answer, left her and the boys standing out on the street – for more than an hour, once, on a freezing late-winter night. She'd called Dragos, gone round to the old apartment, told him what was happening and he'd shrugged and insisted that she must be exaggerating. 'Even your weird brother can't be that fucked up,' he'd said, and Alina had nodded, knowing it was no use; but he was, he was.

She could have called Dragos that day, from the bedroom, but it was Daniela she called – Daniela over in England, in Kent, in a town called Lenbourne, a town with rows of little houses and gardens and cobbled streets, pretty as the oldest, most enduring parts of Bucharest (Alina had never visited – she hadn't had the money for the journey – but she kept a close eye on her sister's Facebook page). The boys were huddled together on their bed, silent for once, watching her, watching and waiting. She had already told Daniela something of what had been going on – had said that Andrei was acting strangely, that she really needed to find their own place – but not the full extent.

'Andrei's gone,' she told her sister. 'He's locked us in the bedroom and he's gone.'

There was a short, loud silence. 'What do you mean by "gone"?'

Alina looked at her boys, sitting there so quietly. Mihai's arm was round his brother; he was four, Gabriel two. It was months, now, since she'd left them alone with Andrei; she'd dropped out of university, was hardly leaving the apartment for fear of not being allowed back in.

'He's gone away for the weekend. On a retreat, he said. Some religious thing. He locked the door and took the key. Said we should all try fasting until he got back. Said it might make us purer before God.'

'Have you called Dragos?' Daniela spoke quickly, urgently; Alina could picture her sister, rising to action, becoming efficient, bold, organised. And even though she was all those miles away, in England, across miles of land and sea, Alina's breathing slowed as she pictured it: Daniela would help them, Daniela would somehow make everything OK.

'Not yet,' Alina said. 'I called you first.'

'Call Dragos.' Daniela was firm. 'And have him call the police. They'll take it more seriously, coming from him, from the father. It's wrong, but it's how it is in that bloody country. The police will be able to break down the door. They'll get you out. Then take the boys to Dragos's, just for the night. You're safer there. I'm going to come over to Bucharest, Alina, OK?

I'm going to fly over with Eddy tomorrow, and you're going to fly back with us. To England. Don't worry about the flights. We'll sort everything out, OK? *Sora mea*, don't worry, it's going to be all right.'

For Eddy

The night Daniela had met Eddy, she wasn't even meant to have been working. It was Lilia's turn: Daniela had done three evenings in a row, had been looking forward to putting her feet up in front of the television. But Lilia had come down with food poisoning – the poor girl had been stuck in the bathroom all morning – so Daniela had agreed to take her shift.

Working in a pub in a pint-sized English seaside town, with its fish and chip shops, its wide grey skies and its wider, greyer sea had not been a part of Daniela's plan. But she'd finished her accountancy degree, and, like so many of her friends, failed to find a job; she'd been working in a bar in Lipscani when she'd seen the advert online. *Bar staff wanted for English pub.* 'Be careful,' Alina had said when she'd told her about it; they all knew the horror stories, the tales of girls who'd merrily boarded buses to England and never come home. But Daniela wasn't stupid; she researched the place, found its website, which seemed real enough. The Anchor looked nice: grey walls, wooden tables, happy young people drinking glasses of wine. She'd sent an email, had a phone interview with the manager, a man named Steve: youngish, friendly, with an accent she'd strained to understand. Scottish, he'd said – though of course the pub wasn't in Scotland but in a small town called Broadstairs, in a part of England called Kent.

'It's not a bad town,' Steve had said. 'Not the most exciting, maybe, but we like it that way. Things can get a bit rowdy on a weekend, but nothing we can't handle. Nothing like Margate.'

Daniela had had no real idea what he was talking about, but she'd thought it all sounded good. A room came with the job, in the flat over the pub: pretty cheap, as far as she could tell, at least by English standards. So when Steve had emailed a few days later, Daniela had written back right away. *Thank you. I am very happy to accept.*

When she'd told her parents, Tata had grumbled, asked what the point had been of them paying all that money for her studies if she was just going off to be a barmaid somewhere else. Daniela had rolled her eyes at him, turned to Mama. 'England!' She'd seized Daniela by the shoulders, kissed her on each cheek. 'Oh, *draga mea*, you're going to have such fun!'

Mama had been right, really: the job was fun. Steve was a decent boss, firm but kind, and the other bar staff were friendly. Daniela shared the flat with Lilia, who was Ukrainian and sleeping with Tamar, the Tunisian chef; and Cristian, who was also Romanian, from Braşov. Cristian liked her, Daniela could tell: liked her like *that*. But she wasn't interested. He reminded her too much of all the boys from home, in particular of Ştefan, who had turned so nasty when she'd told him that she was ending things. A *scorpie*, Ştefan had called her: a *scorpie* who'd been wasting his time. 'Bitch' was the equivalent word in English; Daniela had exchanged swear words with Charlie, the deputy manager, who had worked at The Anchor for as long as anyone could remember, and had, as Steve put it, a 'potty mouth'. No, she wasn't interested in Cristian; she wasn't, Daniela told herself, interested in any men at all.

And then she had met Eddy. About nine o'clock on a Wednesday night, when she wasn't meant to have been working. They weren't usually busy on Wednesdays, had just a couple of bookings, including Eddy's group – a stag do (not his), rare for a weekday. Daniela had noticed Eddy right away, and not only because he stood out – though it was true, there hadn't been many black men in Bucharest, and there weren't many in Broadstairs, either – but because he was so handsome. Tall and muscular, his arms toned and taut under his short-sleeved shirt. She liked the way, too, that he didn't seem to need to dominate the group: he was content to sit back, sipping his beer, watching and listening; speaking sometimes, but mainly taking it all in. There was confidence in that, she felt; there was power in holding back.

At some point during the evening, Daniela had become aware of him watching her, too. They were drunker and louder by then – the groom had begun a game involving many, many shots of tequila. Eventually, Eddy had got up, left the table and come over to the bar, where Daniela was wiping glasses, putting them away for the next day.

'Hi,' he'd said. 'I'm Eddy. I think you're very beautiful. I hope you don't mind me telling you that.'

Daniela put down the glass, the towel. He maintained his steady gaze. He didn't seem drunk in the least. There was something charming, she decided, in the way he'd said what he'd said – not sleazy, not at all, and there was quite a bit of that, even in England, even in a nice pub like this. 'I don't mind. Thank you. I'm Daniela.'

Eddy smiled. His teeth were even, bright white; the smile drew his eyebrows into neat arches. She wondered how old he was: a little older than her, she thought, but not much. Perhaps twenty-five, twenty-six? She was twenty-two.

'Daniela,' Eddy said. 'Maybe I could give you my number, and if you'd like to, you could call me, and let me take you out.'

'I'd like that,' she said, meeting Eddy's eye and holding it, not letting go. 'Yes, I'd like that very much.'

'What's Daddy getting for Christmas?'

They were walking back from school. The light was slipping from the afternoon, though it had hardly brightened at all – one of those leaden English winter days – and the cars were turning on their headlamps, their tyres sending puddles sluicing across the pavement. Angelica was dawdling, as always – stopping to admire the bow-shaped buckles on her shoes; picking a stick up from the ground and dragging it along a set of railings, conjuring a hollow, brittle music.

Daniela fought to suppress her irritation, and failed. She ought to have brought the car – now she had to carry Angelica's nativity play costume – but she'd been indoors all day cleaning and chasing invoices, had wanted a breath of air. And then she'd seen Harriet at the school gates – Harriet Jones, Lily's mum – and Harriet had blanked her again. Well, not completely – she'd turned when Daniela had said her name, offered the briefest, coolest smile. And all because Daniela hadn't seen the WhatsApp message she'd sent, reminding her that Lily was vegetarian; because, unknowing, Daniela had served the kids *sarmale* with minced pork (which Lily had loved, by the way). It had been an honest mistake; was Harriet really never going to let it go? They held grudges, these English women; they were worse than the gangsters in Bucharest.

They passed another broad Victorian house: grey brickwork, chequered path, Christmas tree in the bay window, not a sprig of tinsel in sight. Fran and Adam Lytton's place; Daniela had cleaned the house, and others like it, after she'd first moved in with Eddy. The Lyttons took their cars to Valley Motors – that was how Daniela had heard about the cleaning job – and were good customers, even friends of a sort. A week or so ago, Fran had brought her Audi Q5 to Eddy for its MOT and invited him to their Christmas party.

'Not just *me*, both of us,' Eddy had insisted when he'd told Daniela about it that evening.

'Are you sure?' she had shot back, sounding snappier than she'd intended; it had been a long day, Darius had a cold and had only just settled, an hour after she and Alina had put the kids to bed. 'Maybe she's just trying it on with you. Maybe there isn't a party at all. Or maybe it's a party for *two*.'

Daniela had disliked herself even as she'd said it. Eddy had stared at her for a moment – she dreaded that look of his, that disappointed, sad-puppy look – then turned and left the room. Later, in bed, she'd reached for him and said she was sorry, that they could go if he wanted, she just felt awkward going to a party at a house like that, a house she'd used to clean. And what would she wear; she was too fat for all the smart clothes she'd worn before the children. 'Go naked,' he'd said, reaching for her. 'That would make an impression.' And then, into her neck as he kissed her, 'Forget about it. We won't go if you don't want to.'

Now, Angelica reached for the Lyttons' black wrought-iron railings with her stick, drawing out another dull, discordant din.

'Stop it, Angelica. You know what Daddy's getting for Christmas. We chose that jumper together. You said you liked the colour, remember?'

Angelica turned and looked at her mother, still holding her stick. That morning, Daniela had teased her hair into

87

twin bunches, as the women in the Afro-European hair salon in Maidstone had taught her to do. Her eyes were narrowed, fierce. 'I don't mean from me, Mum, I mean from you. What are *you* getting Daddy? Lily's mum's getting her dad driving lessons. Not, like, for a normal car – of course he can drive one of those already – but for a *racing car*.'

Daniela rolled her eyes. Of course Harriet Jones was spending hundreds of pounds on Roland. She'd been talking about sending Lily and her brother Theo to private school; as far as Daniela was concerned, the sooner she did so, the better.

'That's none of your business, Angelica,' Daniela said, and she took her daughter's hand to hurry her along.

Angelica's question lingered in Daniela's mind through the remainder of the day. Through homework. Through the kids' tea and bath-time and the general fuss that surrounded getting four children into bed in the same room. Eddy was late home – the garage was always busy in the run-up to Christmas. So it was only much later, as they were getting into bed, that Daniela said, 'Are you really sure you don't want anything, Eddy?'

'Want anything?' He looked over at her; he was standing in his boxers, leaning down to remove his socks. Still toned, still gym-fit, only a slight softening at the middle to show that he was no longer in his twenties, that neither of them were. 'Anything for what?'

'For Christmas,' Daniela said. She was sitting on the edge of the bed in her nightie, smoothing on hand cream. She never used to wear anything to bed – neither of them had; it had seemed like something only old people did – but since Alina and the boys had come to live with them they had made this concession, among others. There had been an awkward moment early on when Eddy, bare-naked, had encountered Alina on the landing on his way to the bathroom. Eddy said he didn't know which of them had been more embarrassed.

'You know I said not to bother, babe. There's nothing I need. And we're saving, aren't we? It won't be long now.'

'I know.'

She'd been out to see the new house again earlier in the week; the roof was on, and the guttering, and the workmen were making a start on the interior. Everything was to be white and grey, just like the show-house on the corner plot, with its velvet sofas and fifty-inch television and orchids in pots. They were managing without her inheritance; damn Andrei in Bucharest, still squatting in Mama and Tata's apartment like a spider, refusing to let them sell. He could go to hell, and probably would, for what he did to Alina and the boys, to his own flesh and blood.

Daniela put down her tube of hand cream, watched Eddy as he climbed into bed. 'But it doesn't feel right, not getting you anything.'

He drew his pillow up behind him, lay back against the headboard. 'Really, babe. Honestly. There's nothing I want.'

She slipped into bed beside him, lay down. His hand reached for hers; he lifted it, placed it on his chest. His skin was warm through his T-shirt. She felt his ribcage rise and fall. 'Well,' he said. 'Almost nothing.'

Things had been so easy with Eddy, from the start, that Daniela had struggled, at first, to take him seriously. He called when he said he would; he arrived on time, insisted on driving her the short distance from the flat above The Anchor to the Italian a few streets away, and then, the next time they went out, to another smart restaurant several miles along the coast.

Eddy lived in Lenbourne; Daniela had never been there, and he said it was an old market town, pretty in the centre, though he didn't live in the pretty part. He drove an almost-new BMW, sleek and spotless, and owned his own house, a few streets away from his parents; he was a mechanic, worked in his dad's garage, planned to take over the business when his dad retired.

'Not my biological dad, as you can see,' Eddy said straightforwardly on one of these early dates, producing a photograph from his wallet: a white couple, John and May, middle-aged, smiling, their arms around their taller, darker son. 'But the only dad I've known.'

He'd traced his birth mother – he'd told Daniela all about it, right there in the restaurant, offering her these most intimate facts about himself with such lightness, such trust, that she'd had to bite her lip to prevent herself from telling him to stop, that he oughtn't to trust her, that she wasn't at all the nice girl he seemed to think she was. Even this – his biological mother's giving him up for adoption – Eddy appeared to have forgiven; she lived in Ghana now – Accra – and they were in touch. She'd been sixteen when she'd had him, hardly more than a child herself, with a zealous pastor father, Eddy's grandfather, who'd threatened to throw both her and the baby out on the street. 'She did the right thing,' Eddy said. 'I love my mum and dad very much. They've been wonderful. I've been lucky.'

It was too much for her, all of it: his punctuality, his good looks, the fact that he never seemed to get angry with anyone, about anything; the way he asked her questions and listened to her answers, and didn't try to do anything more than kiss her, didn't even invite her back to his. Daniela retreated, stopped taking his calls, told herself she didn't fancy him, that he was –

as she put it to Alina – 'too nice. Not like a man at all. Like a woman, maybe. Maybe he's gay.'

'Doesn't sound very gay to me,' Alina said.

Alina was twenty then and had been with Dragos for three years: Dragos, who played football every weekend, and computer games when he wasn't playing football, and didn't seem to have any interest in getting a job. This was what they both considered a man to be; this, or Tata – who loved Mama, loved all of them, in his bookish, distracted way, but had never bought Mama jewellery or taken her out for an elegant dinner. Not, at least, as far as either of them knew.

'Maybe,' Alina said, 'that's just what English guys are like.'

'I don't know. I think he's hiding something. Maybe he's married.'

Daniela had confronted Eddy eventually. He'd come into the pub one evening. She hadn't noticed him at first – she'd been taking food orders from a large group – so Charlie had served him, and by the time she'd realised Eddy was there he was sitting at a corner table with a mate, not looking in her direction. He didn't look over at her at all, in fact; Daniela couldn't concentrate, messed up the dinner orders. Eventually she could stand it no longer; she went over while Eddy's friend was outside having a cigarette.

'You are ignoring me,' Daniela said.

Eddy looked up. He wasn't smiling. It struck her that she very much wanted him to smile. 'I thought that's what *you* were doing.'

Daniela opened her mouth, closed it again. After a moment she said, 'Are you married?'

Eddy threw back his head then and laughed: a rich, deep sound bellying up from beneath the collar of his shirt. It was useless; of course she fancied him. She wanted to rip that shirt off his body right there. 'Yeah, I am, Daniela, you found me out. I've got a wife and four kids. No, make that two wives. Three.'

'You are laughing at me.'

He held her gaze. 'I am. Because I'm not like that, Daniela. If you want to find out what I'm like, give me a call. Otherwise, let's not waste our time.'

She waited a week. Eddy didn't call, he didn't text, he didn't come back to the pub. She sent him a text, wrote it three times, deleted each version, then forced herself to hit send. *I want to find out*, she wrote. No reply came; she hardly slept that night, kept checking her phone, but nothing came. By the morning she was furious: who did he think he was, this crazy English man, making her wait like this? She stomped off to the shower, and on her return there it was: a message from Eddy. *Good*, he'd written. *Me too. Come for dinner at mine on your next night off?*

She was tired of pretending. *OK*, she sent back. *Tuesday*.

That night, that Tuesday, in his bed, they'd lain together for a long time, her head in the dip of his arm, her hand tracing the ridges of his stomach. The sex had not been perfect – they'd been shy with each other, fumbling, unsure – but this was: the way their bodies fitted together, the nearness of him, the smell of his skin. There was something oddly familiar about it, something easy, something comforting, like catching the refrain of an old song you haven't thought about in years but that, in the hearing, brings a long-forgotten, childish memory of home.

'Where is she?' Eddy said, failing to whisper. 'I can't see her.'

Heads turned: Daniela kept her voice low. '*Shhh*. She's not on yet. It's Year 2 first. First the shepherds, then the wise women.'

On her other side, in Romanian, Alina said, 'That shepherd looks like he's crapping his pants.'

More heads: one, inevitably, belonging to Harriet Jones. Daniela only just stopped herself from sticking out her tongue. Darius, who was on her lap – the hall was crowded, some of the parents were sitting cross-legged on the floor – put a damp mouth to her ear and said, 'Mummy. I need a wee. I need a wee *now*.'

Darius wasn't in the play. The school took it in turns: this year, the spotlight belonged to Years 2 and 5. Angelica's role as a wise woman – there were no wise men in this version, and the group numbered six rather than three – had demanded weeks of repetition of the same two lines. Daniela had spent five nights, too, making her cloak and crown and sewing plastic gems on to the leotard and leggings Angelica was to wear underneath. Anxiety had plagued her for weeks: the crown might be too big and slip down on to Angelica's neck, choking her; she might trip on her cloak, or the gems might fall off and scatter all over the stage. Fears, really, about anything happening to Angelica that might mark her out as even more different than she already was. Not, Daniela reminded herself now as she tried to squeeze herself and Darius out along the row of knees and bags and winter coats, that Angelica seemed aware of these differences: she was happy and popular, all her teachers said so. For her last birthday, her ninth, giddy on finally being released from all those months of home-schooling and circular walks around the empty, shuttered town, Daniela and Eddy had filled their garden with Angelica's friends. Eddy had hired a bouncy castle, Daniela and Alina had cooked for days, they'd bought boxes and boxes of wine, and even Harriet Jones had admitted that it was the best kids' party she could remember.

Returning from the toilet with Darius, Daniela slipped as

quietly as she could back into the hall. The wise women were up next; there they were, lined up by the steps at the side of the stage. Angelica was at the front of the queue: she was the first wise woman, the leader. Not wanting to disturb the row again, Daniela stayed where she was, at the back by the double doors, holding Darius's hand.

'Look,' she whispered, 'there's your sister.'

'I can't *see*,' Darius said, his face crumpling, and so she lifted him up, bore the weight of him in her arms as Angelica, eyes firmly focused on the nativity scene in front of her – the crib with the doll baby, the foil star, the shepherds, a trio of six-year-olds in tracksuits and stick-on beards – mounted the steps and crossed the stage. Beside the crib, Angelica stopped, her followers almost colliding behind her. Angelica turned to the room in her gold-card crown, her face shimmering under the lights (Daniela had painted her cheeks generously with her best glittery eyeshadow).

'We have come from the East,' Angelica said, her voice loud and steady, carrying clearly even to her mother and brother at the back of the hall, 'bearing gifts.'

Daniela could see Eddy's head turning, scanning the hall, making sure she wasn't missing this; he was holding his mobile at the same time, keeping his hand steady, the camera's eye trained on the stage. His gaze found her, and she waved, and he smiled: that smile, their daughter's smile now, and their son's; the smile she still remembered from the first time she'd seen Eddy in the pub in Broadstairs all those years ago.

Ten years, in fact; they'd celebrated their unofficial anniversary with an Indian takeaway, still under lockdown, Alina disappearing early to her room. Eddy had bought her a necklace, four silver rings joined to a fine chain, each ring engraved with a name: Eddy, Daniela, Angelica, Darius. She'd bought him a bottle of vodka: good vodka, his favourite, Grey Goose. He'd seemed happy enough, had gone straight over and poured them each a shot; but still, Daniela's lack of imagination had shamed her. She was useless at buying presents for Eddy. Everyone else she could manage – the kids; Alina; May and John; the handful of friends she'd made over her years in England – but Eddy's own generosity always seemed to eclipse hers. Each birthday, each Christmas, he presented her with something beautiful, something she loved and would never have thought of buying for herself.

He'd got it wrong only once. The first Christmas they'd shared; they'd only been a couple for a few months, and now they were living together, with a baby on the way. The pregnancy hadn't been exactly planned, but it hadn't exactly not been either. She was happy about it, anyway – they both were. With Eddy, Daniela felt calmer, steadier; it seemed to her that the future made sense now, that the course of things was mapped out before them.

They had spent that first Christmas with Eddy's parents; they'd been welcoming to Daniela, hadn't seemed to think that things were moving too fast. (Unlike Tata, who'd made a huge stink when she'd told him and Mama about Eddy, uttering a series of racial slurs that Daniela could never have imagined coming from her father's lips. She hadn't spoken to him since, hadn't yet told her parents that she was pregnant, and withheld from Eddy the real reason why; Daniela would still not, in fact, have fully forgiven her father four years later, when he and Mama would collide head-on with a drunk driver doing ninety miles an hour in the wrong lane.)

Anyway, there they'd been, that Christmas morning, in John and May's living room. Eddy had stepped out to the car – he'd been secretive about packing the boot, told her not to

95

look inside – and returned with an oversized box, beautifully wrapped in dark-blue patterned paper. 'For the woman I love more than anything in the world,' the label had read. Jewellery, she'd thought with a thrill, hidden inside a bigger box, perhaps, to throw her off the scent; but when Daniela had torn off the paper she'd found not another smaller box, with a diamond necklace inside, but a slow cooker.

'You said you miss your mum's cooking,' Eddy said, grinning. 'Now you can make her lamb stew yourself.'

They still laughed about it now. Daniela's face; Eddy's dawning realisation that he'd made a mistake. But Daniela had used the slow cooker quite a lot in the end; she still did. So really, even that gift hadn't been so far off the mark.

We have come from the East, bearing gifts. What had Daniela bought for Eddy this Christmas? Nothing. Nada. *Nimic.* He'd been saying for weeks that he didn't want a present, but she couldn't, surely, Daniela thought now, holding their son, watching their daughter, take him at his word. Even if Eddy really didn't want her to spend money on him, there must be something she could do to show how much she loved him, valued him, wanted to make him happy. Something other than the obvious.

At the front of the hall, the six wise women edged towards the crib, the doll Jesus, the shepherds in their tracksuits sitting bored and restless on the lip of the stage.

It struck Daniela then, with the clarity of a light switched on: the party. The Lyttons' party. Eddy obviously wanted to go. They hardly ever went out these days – rarely since the kids, even less since the virus. Daniela couldn't even remember the last time they'd been to a party together. Not a smart party, probably with caterers and waiters, in a house that smelt of vanilla and had a bathroom the size of their entire upstairs (Daniela had really loved the Lyttons' house). She could make the effort, couldn't she? Find a dress that still fitted, do her make-up, her hair. Remind Eddy, for a night, of how it had been when they met. Those summer evenings, Eddy waiting for her outside The Anchor: not at the wheel, honking the horn, as Ștefan had used to, but standing, leaning against the passenger door in his shirt and jeans. Watching her walk over to him in her dress, her high heels, the fabric clinging to her thighs. Never taking his eyes off her; making her feel not like an object, a thing to claim as his own, but seen, really seen, as it had seemed to Daniela then that she had never been seen by anyone before.

'This,' Angelica said loudly, brightly, 'is the baby born to be king.'

Yes. A party. Her best dress. His best shirt. The two of them, out together for the evening. Prosecco – maybe even champagne – and those funny little snack things posh English people served at parties. What did they call them? A French word, wasn't it? *Hors d'oeuvres*. Or was it *vol au vents*? Daniela didn't know. She didn't care. Either way: yes. She'd tell Eddy later, say she really wanted to go to the Lyttons' after all. It wasn't much, maybe, but it was something.

Darius squirmed in Daniela's arms, a slippery fish. A heavy one, too. 'Mummy, I want to get *down*.'

Daniela set her son down on the polished floor, took his hand and watched Angelica as she produced a gift from under her cloak – an empty shoe box Daniela had wrapped in silver paper and tied with blue ribbon – and placed it carefully, in silent reverence, at the foot of the doll's crib.

For Jake

He'd missed a call from Jake. Three of them, in fact. He hadn't left a voicemail, but there were several messages – breathless, unpunctuated, as Jake's always were.

How are you mate

Called for a chat

Hope the kids are good, and the missus

Eddy put down the phone. He was making tea; there were three mugs lined up in front of him, each with its own bag of PG Tips. Biscuits on a plate – shortbread, homemade; Jim's wife Pam was a star baker, could go on *Bake Off* if she had a mind to. Eddy might be the boss these days, but he wasn't too grand to do the tea run. And anyway, he liked the moment's breather, away from the workshop, the stereo (they took it in turns; today was Dan's choice, which meant Kiss and Iron Maiden blasting out all day), the grease and oil and queasy petroleum perfume.

The kettle clicked. Eddy poured water into each mug, followed by a slick of milk. Jim liked one sugar (used to be two, but Pam had put her foot down), Dan two. Eddy didn't take any – he spent long enough in the gym keeping the weight off these days. He'd avoid the biscuits, too – or maybe just have the one, so that Jim wouldn't take offence on Pam's behalf.

What was Jake doing right now, out there in the brown field he called home? Ten o'clock – he was probably just up, still in his T-shirt and joggers. Radio 4 on, no doubt; Jake kept it on all day, learnt more that way, he said, than he had in all their years at school. God, he was clever: the boys in their class had called him 'professor', some meaning it more kindly than others. Jake should have had his PhD by now; he should have been warm and comfortable teaching in some university lecture hall rather than half-frozen in a fruit-picker's caravan. He should have been a lot of things, Jake Lamb. It was sad. It was more than sad: it was a proper tragedy.

Just at work, mate, Eddy typed back. *I'll call you later. Stay warm. Cold one today.*

He slipped his phone back into the pocket of his overalls, carried the tray downstairs. He felt his phone go when he was back under Mrs Anderson's Mini Cooper; it was a while before he could reach it and read Jake's replies. Six messages this time.

OK mate
Yeah, will do
Got my long johns on, haven't I
Take care
Don't worry about ringing back
I know you're a busy family man. Brady Bunch ha ha

Eddy couldn't remember, now, how he and Jake had become friends. The kinship of outsiders, he supposed: he the only non-white boy in the class, Jake the only one who didn't wear a coat, or the right uniform.

Or perhaps it was only that their surnames followed each other in the register – Jake Lamb, Eddy Lane – and so they'd found themselves sitting together in their form room from the first week on. They'd become inseparable, a unit of two, pitted against the idiots and thugs who'd roamed the ugly breeze-blocked halls. Some of them were his customers now: guys with families, bringing in their vans for skin-of-the-teeth MOTs. Their schoolboy racism, their thick-headed cruelty had, Eddy believed, been born of ignorance rather than genuine malice. He had tried to forgive it; in most cases he had almost succeeded.

Jake should never have ended up at King Edward's with the other rejects. He should have sailed through the eleven-plus, taken up his rightful place at Lenbourne Grammar, but Jake hadn't even bothered to take the exam. 'Who cares about all that?' he said with a shrug. Eddy did; he'd studied hard, had wanted to show his mum and dad that their investment in him had paid off. They insisted they weren't disappointed, but he knew they were lying; his mum had been telling him, for as long as he could remember, that he could be anything he wanted – a doctor, a lawyer, the prime minister. Now, his dad was talking about bringing him into the garage at weekends, training him up. Eddy didn't mind – he'd been tinkering with engines since he was old enough to hold a spanner – but he couldn't help feeling that on some level he'd let them both down.

Jake didn't have a mum to disappoint: she was dead, had died when he was a baby, some kind of cancer, and his dad didn't give a toss. That was exactly how Jake had put it back then – Eddy could remember it very clearly, the square set of his friend's narrow shoulders, the defiant jut of his chin.

Rick Lamb didn't seem to care very much, it was true. He drove trucks, was away for weeks at a time, leaving Jake with his two older brothers, Kieran and Sean, both of whom had left King Edward's at sixteen. The first time Eddy had gone back to Jake's house for tea – he lived in a pebbledash estate on the fringes of a village outside Lenbourne, close to the motorway – Jake had cooked the meal himself, heating a can of beans in the microwave, toasting the bread, grating orange plastic cheese over the top.

They'd eaten with their plates on their laps, in a living room stacked with engine parts and inner tubes. Sean was into quad-bike racing; Eddy had seen him a few times at Valley Motors, though his dad hated quad bikes, didn't have anything to do with them if he could help it. There was a strong smell of dog; the Lambs had two of them, fat black Labradors who never got enough exercise and sat watching the boys as they ate, their sad chocolate eyes not moving from the plates. After tea, they took the dogs for a walk, trailing along a muddy path through the woods to the clearing where Jake had his den – a grubby tarpaulin slung between two trees, under which he had assembled a pile of mouldering cushions and an assortment of treasures: Top Trump cards, a pair of battered footballs, a book he said had belonged to his mother. *Black Beauty*; it had a blue cover and a picture of a black horse with a white star on its forehead. Jake showed Eddy the writing on the inside cover: *Lisa Sullivan, June 1970.* His mother's handwriting: careful, looped, childish. She'd been the same age then, Jake said, as they were now.

'Don't tell anyone I have this,' Jake said. 'Not my brothers, not anyone. Don't tell anyone it's here.'

'I won't,' Eddy said; he couldn't see why anyone would care, but Jake was staring at him, wide-eyed. Panicked, Eddy thought, though he didn't know why. 'I won't,' he said again. 'I promise.'

The caravan was worse than Eddy remembered. There it was, crouched in the lee of a tall, leafless hedge. The exterior had once been white, he guessed, but was now a scummy green. There was a tarpaulin – memories of that den under the trees – drawn across part of the roof, and one of the windows was missing. Jake had nailed a sheet of plyboard across it, giving the van an uneven, purblind look.

'Christ, mate,' Eddy said. 'Can't Kieran do something about all this? Give you a hand?'

Jake shrugged. He was watching the kids as they made their way across the cold earth; Eddy had told them to go in search of objects for their keepsake boxes, pine cones or stones or a leaf they could press between the pages of a book. Angelica was getting a bit old for this; she'd stared back at him, sullen, looking so much like Daniela when she was in one of her moods that Eddy had had to stifle the desire to laugh. Now she was trailing after Darius, dragging a stick across the rutted mud. It was freezing today, too; the kids couldn't stay out long. Eddy had promised to take them to Starbucks for hot chocolate on the way back. Cream *and* marshmallows: such was the price of their silence.

'Says it's up to me, doesn't he? He's given me the van and the field, the rest is my lookout.'

'I see.'

'Shall we sit in? You can keep an eye on the kids from the back.'

Inside wasn't as bad as out. The place was spartan but clean: twin padded benches; rolled-up duvet; Formica-topped table; mugs drying on a folded tea towel. No Christmas decorations, Eddy saw with relief; he wasn't sure he could have borne the poignancy of a miniature tinsel tree.

The men sat, Eddy watching his children through the back window, now two diminished figures approaching the far hedge.

Eddy looked away, back to Jake, sitting opposite him, a small wooden animal in his palm: a duck, Eddy saw, as Jake lifted his hand to show him.

'For Darius,' he said. 'And look, this one's for Angelica.' Jake reached behind him to a scaffold-board shelf. There were other wooden animals up there, a whole menagerie: cats and dogs and giraffes and what might have been a hippo or an elephant, Eddy couldn't quite tell. Jake picked up one of the cats; it was sleeping, curled in on itself, its closed eyes two tiny, narrow nicks in the smooth surface of the wood.

'Wow, mate. They're beautiful.'

Jake laid the cat down on the table, next to the duck. 'Haven't had a chance to wrap them.'

Eddy looked back to the field; the kids were coming back now, there wasn't much time. 'Don't be silly. That doesn't matter. The kids'll love them.' What would he tell Daniela? He pushed the thought away. 'Listen, mate. How are things? You doing OK?'

There was a long silence, during which Eddy allowed himself to imagine all the confessions that might be about to come his way: all the miniature disasters that, together, constituted the one all-encompassing mess his friend had made of his life. Or what Eddy knew of that life, anyway; they weren't exactly close any more, he hadn't been out to the caravan in, what, six months? Daniela didn't know he was here; she hadn't known the last time he'd come either. Eddy didn't lie to her, he just didn't mention it; but this was the first time he'd brought the kids, which meant asking them to lie to her, or at least not offer the full truth, and that didn't sit right with him, not at all.

'I'm more than OK, mate,' Jake said. 'I've met someone.'

Eddy dragged his gaze away from the field. Jake was smiling: a proper Cheshire Cat grin. 'Met someone?'

Jake nodded. 'Her name's Lizzy. She's . . . amazing. You know what I'm saying. The real deal.'

Eddy laughed then. For Christ's sake. And here he'd been, thinking . . . Well, all sorts. Dark thoughts. Death and disaster. And instead the guy was in love. 'Christ, Jake! That's great! You had me worried there for a sec.'

Jake nodded again, but his smile was slipping from his lips. 'Yeah. Thing is, though, I don't know if . . . You know. She feels the same.'

'You don't know? What, you're not together?'

'No. Not as . . .' His shoulders slumped. 'No. We're not. I mean, look at me. Look at this place. It's a mess. I'm a mess. But I thought maybe you could . . . I don't know. Help. Lend me a bit of that Eddy Lane magic.'

'Daddy! *Dadddyyyyy!*'

'Hang on, mate.' Eddy stood, pushed open the caravan door; there were Angelica and Darius, his son leading, carrying a grey-black hunk of hacked-out tree. 'Daddy, look what I found! Look how many circles there are! That means it's really really *old!*'

'It's really dirty and heavy.' Angelica still had that stony face on; Eddy knew she didn't really want to be here, that she wanted to be at home in the warm trying on her nativity play costume. She was a wise woman (the school had done away with the men in this version) and only had two lines, but she spoke them well, clearly and confidently, had been practising for weeks. 'I told him not to pick it up.'

'That's good dirt,' Jake said, 'and good wood, too. Silver birch. Came down a few weeks ago in the storms. Chopped it myself.'

Two pairs of dark-brown eyes watched him, unabashed. 'We're going to see an old friend of mine,' Eddy had told the kids earlier, in the car. 'You've met him before, you just don't remember. It was a while ago.'

'Did you use an axe to chop it?' Darius said now, and Jake nodded. 'I did. And I used it to chop up some of the pieces really small, too, and then I used them to make these.' He opened his fist; there were the duck and the cat, nestled in the dip of his palm.

'Take 'em,' Jake said, handing the duck to Darius, the cat to Angelica. 'They're yours. Happy Christmas.'

The children examined the wooden animals, turning them over in their hands.

'It's not Christmas yet,' Angelica said. 'Not for another week. And it's not wrapped. It's not a proper Christmas present if it's not wrapped.'

'Angelica.' Sharper than he meant to be, but Eddy hated how she sounded: so entitled, so ungrateful. She was only nine, she didn't mean it. She wasn't a brat, he knew she wasn't, but Jake didn't, couldn't, know. 'That's rude. Say thank you.'

She pouted, but she said it, and Darius did, too, with more enthusiasm. 'Mine's a *duck*! A tiny duck made from a tree!'

'I'd better get them back,' Eddy said. 'Their mum'll be back from Bluewater soon. It's getting cold, too. Couldn't you get a wood-burner in here?'

'Could, mate. I could.' Jake didn't say, *with what cash, exactly?*, and Eddy cursed himself silently. Tactless, bloody tactless. Aloud, he said, 'Look, you don't need my help with this woman, Jake. You're all right as you are. You're a good bloke. I know that, and I've known you longer than most. She'd be lucky to have you.'

'Yeah, right, mate. Cheers.' Jake smiled thinly. 'Cheers for coming by. Merry Christmas. I'll be seeing you, Eddy, all right?'

It wasn't that Eddy and Daniela didn't ever argue, exactly; more that they'd learnt, over time, to divert disagreements before they became full-blown rows.

The scale and intensity of the first argument they'd had about Jake had therefore come as a shock. His release date had been set; he'd written to Eddy to tell him, asked if they could meet once he was out. They'd exchanged letters a few times while Jake had been away – Jake's always far longer than Eddy's, but then, he was the one with all that time on his hands – but hadn't actually seen each other since the December of 2008, the first Christmas Jake had spent in prison.

Guilt about not having gone to visit Jake more than once during his years inside had hung heavily over Eddy; he'd told himself that it wasn't his fault, he was so busy with work, and they'd moved Jake twice, first to Birmingham and then to somewhere up north. A nightmare for his family, or at least it would have been, had they bothered to visit: Jake said in his latest letter that only Kieran had come, that their dad didn't want anything at all to do with him. *Kieran knows it was an accident,* Jake wrote, his handwriting blunt, oversized, a child's writing, Eddy thought, not that of a full-grown man. In some ways, in his mind, Jake was still that boy he'd known at school: skinny, scruffy, wearing the crest of the wrong school. *I guess Dad's still angry. Anyway, I have to look forward, not back. That's what they all tell me in here.*

'No,' Daniela had said when Eddy told her Jake was getting out, asked whether he might come over to the house to meet her and Angelica. Maybe stay for a few days, just while he got back on his feet. 'No way. Are you mad? Have you gone completely crackers?'

Daniela used some funny English idioms – she'd learnt some from her mum, who'd spent a year in Manchester in the 1980s, and others from Charlie, a leathered old Kent native with a mouth like a navvy, who'd worked with Daniela at The Anchor in Broadstairs. Eddy sometimes teased her about it; looking at his wife's face then – her furious glare – he had understood that this ought not to be one of those times. 'He's a friend of mine, babe. A good friend. Or he used to be, anyway. And he's had a tough time. I'd like to help him out.'

She had lifted her chin, mulish, unbending. 'Eddy! He's been in prison. He *killed* someone. His own brother. And you want to bring him here, to our home, to meet our baby girl? When I'm pregnant, too?'

Eddy had taken a breath. It was evening; they'd just finished dinner, Angelica, then seven months old, had finally submitted to a deep, dummy-soothed sleep. Daniela was eight weeks into the new pregnancy; they hadn't told anyone yet except Alina, over in Bucharest; they had only just found out themselves.

'It wasn't Jake's fault,' Eddy said. 'I've told you what happened. It was an accident. A terrible accident. He's done his time, and now he has no one, Daniela. No one at all.'

Daniela smoothed her hair back off her face. 'If it wasn't his fault, why did the judge put him in the prison? Why was he – how do you say – off his face on *drugs*?' She stood up, put a hand to the soft pad of flesh at her middle – the deflated swell of her previous pregnancy, not the rising mound of this one: it was too early yet for her to be showing. 'And why is this your problem, anyway? Why didn't you go to see him in prison, if he is such a good friend, as you say?'

Guilt rose, bitter-tasting, in Eddy's throat. The unfamiliar tang of anger, too. 'It's not that simple, Daniela. I did go.'

She shook her head. 'You said you went to see him once, Eddy. You went once, and now you want to bring this guy, this criminal, here, to our home, and I'm saying no. No way.

I don't want you to see him. I don't want you to talk to him. I don't want you having nothing to do with him.'

He'd lost it then, lost it in a way he couldn't remember ever having lost it; certainly not with Daniela. It was the fact she was forbidding him from doing something, saying who he could or couldn't see; there surely had to be a limit. He'd shouted at her, she'd shouted back, for a long time, too long; they'd woken Angelica, and Daniela had rushed upstairs. He'd sat in the kitchen while Daniela comforted her, listening on the baby monitor; his daughter's sobs subsiding, his wife singing softly to her in Romanian. She was pregnant and sleep-deprived – Angelica still woke at least twice at night – what was he thinking, shouting at her like that? What kind of man was he? He talked sternly to himself, sobering by degrees; by the time Angelica had settled and Daniela come back downstairs, Eddy was calm again.

'I'm sorry, babe. I'm really sorry. You're right. I won't bring Jake here. I won't see him. Not if you feel this strongly about it. You guys are the most important thing. Just you. Nobody else.'

He'd meant it, too; and it would have stayed that way, he thought, if he hadn't bumped into Jake in town, a long time after his release – Eddy hadn't written back, and Jake hadn't written again or called; Eddy had heard through someone who knew Kieran that Jake hadn't come back to Lenbourne, had decided to stay up north.

It was a summer Sunday afternoon; Eddy had taken Angelica and Darius to the playground, giving Daniela some time to rest. He'd just bundled Darius back into his pushchair, was leaning down to fasten the strap, when he looked up and saw him: Jake Lamb, sitting on a bench just a few feet away, reading a book.

Eddy contemplated turning away, pretending he hadn't noticed him. But Angelica chose that moment to scream about something – that he wouldn't let her have an ice cream, probably – and Jake looked up from his book, and their eyes met. He didn't smile, but he didn't *not* smile, either. Jake stood up, slid the book into his pocket. He was taller than Eddy remembered; skinny as ever, though. His hair was longer, almost to his shoulders. He looked older; he was, of course. They both were.

'All right, mate?'

Eddy nodded. Angelica issued another of her ear-splitting screams. 'Angelica, wait a minute. Daddy's talking.'

Jake shook his head. 'Nah, won't hold you up. She's lovely. They both are.'

Eddy nodded again. He didn't seem to be able to speak, couldn't think of any way to narrow what seemed, in that moment, an unbridgeable distance between them.

'Here.' Jake reached into his pocket, took out the book – *The Road*, by someone called Cormac McCarthy – and tore off a strip of paper. From his other pocket he produced a pen. 'Take my number. I know you're . . . Well. It's been a long time. Dad's gone. Maybe you heard. Heart attack. Kieran's farming now, out towards Waddington. Said I could stay there for a while. Got a caravan. Help with the picking, you know.' He handed Eddy the slip of paper with his number on it. Both the children were silent now, watching him, this stranger giving his phone number to their dad. 'Call me if you want, Eddy. I get it if I can't come to the house. Maybe you could come and see me some time.'

Eddy took the piece of paper, looked down at the scrawled digits and back at the face of his old friend. 'Yeah, mate. Maybe I could.'

He thought about it for a couple of days; held the idea in his mind, examined it from every angle. The car wasn't worth much; he'd taken it off old Lenny Dimmock for a few quid as a favour, to save him the trouble of selling it for scrap. They might get a few parts out of it, but that wasn't really their line of work; Eddy had already called a bloke he knew, over on the island, said he was shut for Christmas now but he'd be through in the new year. It still ran all right – or would do, if Eddy worked on it for a bit. Old Lenny just hadn't had the cash to put it through its MOT.

On Tuesday evening, Eddy stayed late – texted Daniela to let her know – and did what needed to be done. Shaved rust from the chassis, applied wax oil; replaced the cam-belt and the brake pads. It wasn't a bad old motor – a Ford Fiesta, 04 plates; with a bit of TLC, it could be good for at least another year. He wondered how Jake got around at the moment – cadged lifts from Kieran, maybe, or walked the mile or so to the bus stop in Waddington. It was no way to live; the lack of a car, perhaps, was the least of it, but it would be something, wouldn't it. Yes, it would. He could take this Lizzy out somewhere: the island maybe, or Margate, or the wild flatlands over at Dungeness. Wind in their hair. Stroll by the sea. You needed wheels out here if you were trying to impress a woman. Old-fashioned, maybe, but there it was.

It was after eleven by the time Eddy got home. The lights were off in the front bedrooms and he let himself in quietly, carefully. Went through to the kitchen for a cuppa and found the lights on, and Daniela sitting at the table. She looked up, and he saw them: the duck and the cat, Jake's wooden animals. Oh God. Eddy had put them in the pocket of Darius's blue coat on Sunday while they were in Starbucks and then forgotten about them. Darius had worn that coat to school today, he must have found them and shown his mother. *Mummy, Daddy's friend gave these to us. He lives in a caravan in a field. He has an axe. He chopped down a tree.*

'How is he?' she said.

Eddy swallowed. All right, so the game was up. 'OK, I think. The place is a dump. Kieran won't help him fix it up, and he doesn't have any money to do it himself. It's like Kieran's still punishing him.'

Daniela held his gaze. Her eyes, in the electric glare, seemed to carry an unnatural, glossy sheen. She didn't seem angry; more quiet, thoughtful. Eddy breathed a little more easily. 'But he gave him somewhere to live.'

'Yeah. An old caravan. For the fruit-pickers, you know.'

She nodded. 'And he made these for the kids?'

'He did.'

Daniela nodded again. Eddy went over to the kettle, filled it from the tap, replaced it on its stand. Without turning round he said, 'I'm sorry I didn't tell you.'

She sighed. After a moment she said, 'It's all right. I'm glad, actually . . . I'm glad that he is OK. He has suffered enough, I think.'

'He has.' Eddy listened to the water gurgle and hiss. He still had his overalls on; he smelt, he knew, of grease and oil and sweat. Relief coursed through him: relief that she knew, that there was nothing between them left unspoken. He'd drink his tea, have a shower, climb into bed, feel the soft, scented warmth of her body beside his. 'I've been working on a motor for him. Bit of an old banger, failed its MOT. But I can make it run. He doesn't have a car, and he's all the way out in the country. Thought I'd give it to him. Seeing as it's Christmas.' He turned, leaning back against the counter, waiting for the water to boil. 'That is, if you don't mind.'

Daniela picked up the wooden duck, held it in her palm, as if measuring the weight of it, the size and scale. 'I don't mind. It's a good thing to do.' She looked up at him again. 'You are a good man, Eddy. A kind man. The best.'

Eddy smiled. The kettle clicked. 'I'm not, really. But I try.'

For Lizzy

Lizzy wasn't there when he arrived. The trestle table with its tea urn, its packets of economy supermarket biscuits. The round tables and plastic chairs, set out at regular distances, as if for a wedding or a children's party. Jake scanned it all and failed to find her.

Parachute held its twice-weekly meetings – *Having a tough time? Struggling with your mental health? Just need some company? Drop in for a cup of tea and a chat* – at Jackson's, the old creekside brewery. The company was long gone, defeated by a brasher, younger rival which now supplied most of the pubs in the south-east. Jake remembered the building as derelict, a local eyesore – though he hadn't seen it as ugly himself, had found a kind of brave beauty in its high, smokeless chimneys and crumbling red brick. They'd come down here as kids sometimes, he and Sean and Kieran, riding over on their bikes, his brothers leading the way, him trailing behind. Chicken, they'd called him, when he'd been too afraid to climb over the hoardings. They'd left him watching the bikes, listening out for security guards or police; though no one, as Jake recalled, had ever come.

Now the place had been renovated, tarted up; there was a café downstairs, posh, overpriced coffee and artisanal flatbreads (whatever they were), and upper rooms rented out to freelances and artists and community groups. The library was here now, too; Jake spent a lot of his time there, they knew him, didn't mind if he hung around for a while with a paperback, a newspaper, a magazine. They'd made a nice courtyard outside, where the old stables used to be, with tables you could sit at when the sun shone, just sit and read and not have anyone trying to make you buy anything, trying to move you on.

They locked the tables away in winter, but there was a bench you could sit on if you were hardy enough, which Jake was. He was checking the yard now from one of the tall, metal-framed windows in case Lizzy was down there, maybe running late; but no, just an old guy in a cap and winter coat shuffling across the cobbles with his library books in a plastic bag. Another regular. Sam, the library assistant, sometimes made the old man a cuppa; she sometimes made one for Jake, too.

'You all right there, Jake?'

Patricia: sixty-ish, stocky, with a hairstyle that looked as if she'd put a pudding bowl over her head and cut round it with secateurs. Kind, in her brisk, bustling way. She did a lot of volunteering, helped run the community cinema, was always trying to get him to join in. Jake knew her type; the prison librarian, Jane, up in Leeds had been similar, making time for him, ordering in the books he liked. Novels, the ones with bare, whittled sentences, the ones whose authors didn't waste words. McCarthy, Carver, Hemingway.

'No Lizzy today?' he said, trying to keep his voice light – no snow today, then? He could see that Patricia wasn't convinced.

'She's not in today, Jake. Called in sick. Says she'll be here next week for the Christmas do. You are coming, aren't you?'

Jake looked back to the window, the yard; the old man had gone, the scene was bare, an empty stage. Someone had hung Christmas lights from the wood-framed portico; they were on now, a string of bulbs glowing in the grey dullness of a December afternoon.

'Yeah,' he said. 'I'll be here.'

Patricia left him alone after that, which was something. Jake got himself a cup of tea and a bourbon biscuit – it was either that or a fig roll, someone always got to the jammy dodgers first – and sat back on his window seat, not quite wanting to commit to the room. Busy today – Christmas had that effect on people. It had always been the hardest time in prison: more fights than usual; even guys who were usually pretty calm could turn nasty over nothing – a meal that wasn't hot enough, a joke that hadn't quite hit home. He'd once seen a bloke he'd held to be one of the most even-tempered on the wing lose his crap over his turkey dinner, grab the guy next to him and put his hands around his neck. Hadn't got very far with that – the canteen was the last place to start anything, there were officers everywhere – and the bloke had broken down as they held him back, started blubbing like a child. Harris, his name was. Michael Harris. Everyone called him Mickey. Had four kids, hadn't even met one of them, she'd been born while he was inside. Christmas was always hardest in there for the guys with kids.

'How's it going, Jake?' Sally, this time, coming over with her neat blonde fringe and her mug of herbal tea. She was wearing a festive jumper: navy, with a white woven pattern of berries and holly leaves. 'Doing anything nice for Christmas?'

He shrugged. She meant well – ran the charity, didn't she; had recruited Lizzy as a volunteer, and for that he was more than grateful – but really, what was there to say? What planet was she on? Scrap that, he knew: she lived on Church Street, in one of those lovely old houses, half-timbered, Christmas wreaths on all the doors. He'd walked there with her once after a meeting, when they'd happened to be going the same way. Caught a glimpse inside as she pushed open the door – the creamy paint, the gold-framed pictures, the smiling husband coming down the thickly carpeted stairs to greet her.

'Not really,' he said. 'Might have my dinner at my brother's.' He wouldn't, if he could help it – would far rather stay in the van with a microwave lasagne and his book – but Kelly might insist. And he knew that Sally would rather not picture him alone – didn't want her passing this pathetic image on to Lizzy either, not that Jake could allow himself to imagine that they spent any of their time discussing him.

Sally nodded, encouraging. 'That's good. You doing OK, then? I know it's not always the easiest time of year . . .'

She trailed off. A renewed sense of hopelessness came over him, a rolling fog. He'd spent all week looking forward to seeing Lizzy – not even speaking to her necessarily, but just being in the room with her, being reminded that she existed, that the world contained her too. Now she wasn't coming, and there was another whole week to endure.

'Lizzy,' Jake said. 'She all right, is she? Patricia said she's not feeling too well.'

Sally looked at him, her head on one side. She wasn't stupid, that one. But then, they probably all knew he was a little in love with her, didn't they? Everyone except Lizzy herself.

'It's a hard time of year for her too,' Sally said. 'I think you know why. I think she's told you, hasn't she? About her mother?'

He nodded. 'Yeah.'

'I'll let her know you were asking after her, if you like.'

Her voice was warm, educated. Not local. Lizzy's voice was like that, too; she'd grown up round here, like him, but she'd been to the grammar school, and then to university in Bristol, stayed there for a few years before coming back to Kent. Jake loved the way Lizzy spoke – softly, and slightly halting, as if not quite trusting the through-line of her own thoughts. He loved to listen to Lizzy speak. He played the sound of her voice over in his mind sometimes, just to hear its own particular music.

He'd had girlfriends; he wasn't a complete no-hoper. Well, not in that way. They got started young where he was from: Kieran had taken up with Kelly when they were fourteen, and Jake had lost his virginity at thirteen, to a girl two years older who lived at the other end of the village. Her dad had found out, come after Jake; Sean had squared up to him, until the guy had decided it wasn't worth it and cleared off. Jake had had to give that part of the village a wide berth for some time – not easy in a place the size of Westling, which was basically just a string of houses and a pub. As Sean had said, though, he didn't know what the girl's dad was getting so het up about anyway; it wasn't as if Jake had been her first.

Jake had always liked Sean more than Kieran. He wasn't sure whether that was how you were meant to feel about your own brothers, but that was how it had been. Sean was more like their mum than their dad, everybody said so: he had her dark hair, her blue Irish eyes. Kieran and Jake were sandy-blond and wiry, like their dad. Jake had wondered, in his darker moments, whether things would have been different – whether he'd have felt differently – if it had been Kieran he'd hit that night, rather than Sean. He didn't think so – a brother was a brother, after all; a life was a life – but sometimes he wondered.

There was a girl Jake had been seeing when it happened. Lisa, her name was, same as his mum; he'd thought this was a good sign, that they were meant to be together, maybe. He was twenty-three, clueless, working as a labourer: farm work, construction, whatever was on offer. His dad had wanted Jake to follow him on to the roads, driving trucks, as Sean was doing, too – but Jake couldn't stand that, preferred being outside; sun on his back, and wind and rain, but he didn't mind, better that than a stuffy cab stinking of burgers and stale air.

He was still living at home, if that was the right word for it, though both of his brothers had moved on by then – Sean to a flat in Lenbourne, Kieran and Kelly to a rented cottage on the farm Kieran was managing. Their dad's house was still a dump, but at least Jake often had the place to himself. They'd spent a lot of time up in his room, he and Lisa, doing the usual, as well as drinking and smoking weed – Lisa's brother was a small-time dealer – and then, gradually, doing other stuff. Coke, ketamine, mushrooms, MDMA. Jake had tried most of them before but Lisa was really into it, ketamine especially. Jake liked it, too; a couple of bombs, a few vodka shots and the hard corners of the world seemed to soften, its boundaries fracture and dissolve. They spent hours together, watching DVDs, lying in a tumble of limbs. Wandering out through the woods behind the house, to the place where Jake had once had his den; the place he used to go as a child when he missed his mother and just wanted to sit alone for a while, thinking of her, remembering her smell, her touch, the weight of her curtain of hair across his face when she'd laid him down to sleep.

Jake didn't do drugs as often as Lisa did – she didn't have a proper job, he suspected now that she'd been running supplies for her brother – but enough to turn up late for work a few times too often, to lose one job, then another. He stopped caring; perhaps he never had. There was the life he might have had if his mother was alive, and there was the one he was stuck with; he could read as many books as he wanted, watch as many films as he liked and nothing would ever change. He wasn't Eddy Lane, with his nice parents and their nice house and his nice girlfriends and his cushy job working for his dad. Jake preferred to step out of his own life while he could, if only for a few hours at a time; a line of powder, a twist of cigarette paper, the soft, yielding curves of Lisa's body, the warm lick and tug of her rough cat's tongue.

The night it happened, they'd both been high as helium balloons. 'Let's nick one of your brother's bikes,' Lisa had said, 'take it for a spin.' It had seemed like a great idea at the time; Jake guessed you'd had to be there, you'd had to be off your face. Sean had two quad bikes then, stored in a lock-up opposite his block. Jake had a key – he kept his tools in there, and some of his and Lisa's stash, too, not that Sean had known anything about that. It had been so easy – they'd driven over in Lisa's car, opened the garage, shoved a screwdriver into the ignition of the bike closest to the door. Hadn't reckoned on the noise, though, had they – too high for that, too high and too stupid. It was 3 a.m. A light went on in Sean's flat; he'd come running out in his T-shirt and boxers, barefoot. Jake was backing the bike out of the garage. The noise of the souped-up engine was deafening, and his mind wild; he hadn't seen Sean, hadn't heard him, hadn't seen him, hadn't heard. Then Lisa had started screaming, and more lights had come on in other flats, and somebody Jake didn't know had come running out with a phone, calling an ambulance, and more people had gathered, and there had been a terrible silence when Jake cut the engine, a terrible silence and his brother lying there on the ground, his feet bare and pale in the darkness.

He'd told Lizzy all of this; well, some of it; as much as he felt she could handle. He rarely spoke of any of it any more, hadn't since prison; what was the point, he was only torturing himself, going over and over how stupid he had been, how selfish and reckless, how much he hated himself. Nobody wanted to hear about it in there, anyway; they all had stories of their own, things they wished they hadn't done, or had done differently. (It was the ones who didn't regret anything that you really had to watch out for.) And back home, most people knew about it, and had already made up their minds about him; that was one of the reasons he'd decided to stay up north for a while, keeping anonymous, lying low.

No, Jake generally didn't talk about what had happened, not to anyone; but Lizzy, well, Lizzy was different. He'd known it from the moment he'd seen her at the meeting, standing there by the table, spreading biscuits on a plate. Not tall, not short, not skinny, not fat; not particularly beautiful, he supposed, in a model kind of way, but when she'd turned and looked at him his breath had stilled in his throat.

'Tell me about yourself, Jake,' Lizzy had said – not that first time, but a few weeks later. 'How are you doing, really?'

There was something about her face – its openness, perhaps; the clarity of her blue eyes (Irish blue); their absolute lack of guile – that made it impossible to lie to her. So he hadn't lied; he'd told her about himself, about who he was, what he'd done, what he had to live with now, the shadow of it falling across everything, blotting out the light. She'd listened. Her eyes had never shifted from his face. When he was done, they'd sat in silence, and he'd been grateful for it, grateful for the fact that she hadn't tried, like others, to reach for some truism, some tired cliché about how we all make mistakes, that time heals all wounds, that true peace comes only when we forgive ourselves. Lizzy had said none of that; and neither had she sat there judging him, as others did – he could tell she wasn't doing that from the cast of her face. She'd just sat there with him for a while, saying nothing, honouring the truth of what had happened and could not be undone.

He'd wanted to give Lizzy something for Christmas: something simple, something beautiful, to show her how grateful he was for the time they'd spent talking together, week after week. For the way she listened, the things she said, the way she smiled at him. For the fact she had trusted him enough to share the truth of her own loss, her own sadness: her mother's death, her return to Lenbourne to see to her mother's things. 'Estate', Lizzy said, which made Jake think of big houses, *Downton Abbey*; but no, she said, the house was just a cottage, out on the Westling Road. (Westling! To think that she had grown up there, just a few miles away from him, just a few years younger, and he had never known.)

She was an only child, she said; there was only her to see to everything. She hadn't mentioned a father, and Jake had seethed at the man, whoever he had been: that he could have brought such a person into the world and then abandoned her. But perhaps that was not how it had happened: perhaps her father had died too; or perhaps he'd never been in the picture, perhaps her mother had decided from the first to go it alone, every bit as bright and beautiful and determined as her daughter seemed to Jake now. Lizzy hadn't said, and he hadn't asked, not wanting to pry, understanding that there were reasons everyone had for keeping some things to themselves.

He loved her, of course; he loved her and she didn't know it. He didn't think she did, anyway; he didn't want her to know – not now, not yet. Perhaps not ever. What was the point: he was Jake Lamb, an ex-con who'd killed his favourite brother by accident, while he was high: a useless waste of space who lived in a caravan and had made a grand cock-up of this one shining gift of a life. He didn't want anyone to know, though he suspected that Sally and Patricia had guessed – not difficult, he supposed, given the way he looked at her; he could hardly believe that Lizzy didn't seem to have worked it out for herself. Or perhaps she had, and she was papering over her inevitable disgust with kindness, with pity; but Jake didn't think so, she didn't seem capable of such dissembling.

He hadn't meant to tell Eddy about Lizzy. He really hadn't meant to, but it was tough keeping joy to yourself, joy and love, almost as tough as sitting on your pain and self-disgust. And there was the way Eddy looked at him – he was sure he didn't mean to, but he still did it, everyone did: they all stared at him with that particular blend of bewilderment and curiosity. *How could you have done this to him, and to yourself? How can you live with it? What is it like to be inside your skin?* Eddy had sat here in the caravan, looking at him like that, and so Jake had told him. *I've met someone.* Made it sound as if something was happening between them, hadn't he – or was about to happen. And he'd seen his friend's face change; Eddy had lost that other look and replaced it with one of surprise, and maybe happiness, and a trace of something else, something Jake hadn't seen in a long time. Respect, he thought. Yes, respect: a man looking at another man and seeing something other than a failure.

So yes, Jake had wanted to give Lizzy some kind of gift; he'd pondered it for ages, saved up a bit of cash from the odd jobs he'd had through the autumn – bit of farm work, for Kieran and others; some scaffolding, some decorating, helping a mate of his brother's repaint the weatherboarding on a sheltered housing block in town. Had even borrowed Kelly's car – she let him sometimes, said they didn't need to bother with insurance long as he made sure he drove like an old lady – and driven over to Bluewater, to that chrome-and-glass shopping centre squatting like a spaceship where a disused quarry had once been. Wandered its aisles as if he were the alien; the lights, the smells, the people eating fried chicken, sipping takeaway coffees, striding in and out of shops, carrying bags of stuff. So much stuff. Jake hadn't known where to start; he had darted into a clothes shop, women's clothes, jeans and jumpers and clingy tops glittering under strip-lights. Caught a glimpse of himself in a mirror: a skinny, haggard bloke, his best denim jacket grubby and faded, his hair hanging lankly to his shoulders. Made an effort, hadn't he – shaved that morning with his pocket mirror, carefully, taking his time, as he did before each Parachute meeting now. It was useless: he still looked like shit. A tramp. A deadbeat. He should get out of here before he frightened some poor passing child.

He had got out, driven home. Left Kelly's car outside the cottage and wandered back across the fields, frost clinging to the mud and the leafless trees, two of the farm dogs running at his heels. It was the dogs that had made him think of it, think of her (not that she was ever far from his mind, these days). Lizzy had two, didn't she – a greyhound and an ancient collie – her mother's dogs. She'd shown him photos on her phone; she left them with her godmother, out the other side of Waddington, when she came to meetings. They couldn't be left alone, she said, they were missing her mum too much; it was lucky she could do her job from home.

Jake had been doing some wood-carving recently, some whittling. Animals, mainly; it was something to pass the time and he was getting better at it, was thinking about trying to sell them, maybe getting a market stall. He'd carve a pair of dogs for Lizzy, a collie and a greyhound; wrap them, call them a Christmas present. Wait for the look on her face when she opened the paper and saw what he had made for her.

The car was there when Jake woke up. He pushed open the door in his dressing gown, and there it was: a Ford Fiesta, dark blue, 04 plates, seen better days, but clean, its paintwork and windows spotless. A bow on the bonnet, and a card, and a set of keys, attached to a pewter key ring shaped like Big Ben.

Confusion slowed his responses. What the hell? Who'd driven out here and left their car right by his caravan? How had he not heard the engine? He didn't usually sleep well – lightly and fitfully as a prey animal, a habit acquired during his time inside – but the previous night he'd taken a couple of tablets for his cold; they must have knocked him out. Jake stepped down on to the field in his slippers. The card showed a snowy scene, cottages blanketed with snow, a red postbox, a robin: a Hallmark version of the English countryside, with none of its casual cruelty and mess. Just yesterday, he'd passed a dead fox on the road, its red coat dusty, matted with blood, its black eyes dull, unseeing.

Merry Christmas, the message read inside the card. *A gift for you, mate, with love from Eddy, Daniela, Angelica and Darius.*

PS It's a bit of an old banger, but I've worked on it – it should see you through a year at least. Take that Lizzy out somewhere nice.

Bloody hell, Eddy. For God's sake. Jake stood for a moment, just staring. Then he picked up the keys, opened the door and climbed inside. The upholstery was worn, the dashboard scuffed, but it smelt fresh, with a faint citrus trace; there was an air freshener in the shape of a lemon hanging from the mirror. Paperwork on the passenger seat, and a certificate of insurance:

Eddy had thought of everything. Jake closed his eyes, leant his head back against the headrest. When he opened them again his cheeks were damp, and he reached up to dry them with his sleeve.

Jake drove into Lenbourne that evening, fresh as his new car in his best shirt and jeans. He parked outside Jackson's, went in carrying Lizzy's present in a plastic bag, feeling better than he had in months, years even: he could have floated up the stairs, feather-light. The decorations were up – tinsel, paper chains, a tree – and there was Christmas music on, old classics – the Rat Pack, Frank Sinatra or Dean Martin, one of that lot anyway, crooning away about letting it snow. And there she was, this time, right in the centre of the room, a glass of wine in her hand.

Lizzy turned. She saw him. She smiled. Jake's world spun and righted itself once more.

Later, when the party was coming to an end – a couple of the older guys had drunk too much, started a bit of a row; Sally had tactfully turned the lights on, suggested they all call it a night – Jake found Lizzy by the booze table, packing soiled glasses into crates.

'Come outside with me,' he said.

He watched her hesitate. 'I'm needed here . . .'

'Please. It won't take long.'

'All right. Just for a bit.'

She followed him downstairs, out across the courtyard to the car park. Thick winter darkness; the low murmur of the party winding down upstairs. 'Jake, what is this?' she said, and he worried for a moment that he'd overstepped – she was, after all, following him into ever-deeper shadows. When they reached his car, he stopped and said, 'I just wanted to show you this. It's mine. My mate gave it to me today, for Christmas. Can you believe it?'

He couldn't see her face, but he heard her cry of surprise. 'Wow, some mate! That's amazing, Jake! Let me see inside.'

Jake turned the key, stepped in, leant over and opened the passenger door. Lizzy climbed in beside him. He switched on the headlamps and the interior light; she closed her door against the cold. They had never been alone before; he was nervous suddenly, aware of the black night surrounding them, concerned again that she would misinterpret his intentions. He only wanted to give her the wooden dogs – he still had them here with him, hadn't yet found a chance to hand them over – and show her the car, give her some idea, perhaps, that he wasn't a complete and utter loser. That someone had cared about him enough, at least, to do him this great, extravagant kindness.

For a while, neither of them spoke. Then he said, 'I wanted to give you this.'

He handed her the gift, in its tissue wrapping, its plastic bag. Lizzy took the bag and looked at him, her face lovely in the dim yellow light. 'Jake. Thank you. I haven't . . .'

He shook his head. 'You didn't need to. I just wanted to . . . Say thanks, I guess.'

'For what?'

'For listening. For talking. It's meant a lot to me.'

Lizzy turned her face away, stared out through the windscreen. He watched her profile: the long lashes, the gentle slant of her nose. How could he ever have thought her less than entirely beautiful? 'And to me, Jake.'

There was another silence, and as it stretched Jake began to allow himself to hope, to imagine himself reaching out and taking her hand, holding it in his. The simplicity of that. The start of something. He could really see himself doing it – his hand was actually shifting towards her – when she said, 'Listen, Jake, I like you. And I don't mean to sound presumptuous – I mean, perhaps you're not thinking in this way anyway, so if you're not, I'm sorry. But I think that maybe . . . I think I need you to know that I can't get involved with you. Romantically, I mean.'

Her words fell heavily. Jake returned his hand to his lap. 'Yeah. I get it. I wasn't . . . I mean, I didn't mean to . . .'

She looked at him again. She smiled. Sadly, he thought, or maybe it was just his own sadness speaking, the shadow of it falling across his vision. 'It's not who I am, Jake.'

Suddenly, he understood. It didn't make the disappointment any less deep, but he understood. Jake nodded. He swallowed again. What an idiot he was. What a fool. He sat up straighter in the driver's seat, gripping the wheel with both hands. Drew a breath, and said, 'I really like talking to you, Lizzy. Maybe we could just hang out a bit outside the meetings, go out somewhere in the car. A walk by the sea, like. Whitstable or Folkestone. It's nice there these days. Posh. As friends. You know what I mean?'

In the passenger seat beside him, he felt her body relax, a breath let go.

'I do know,' Lizzy said. 'I'd like that, Jake.'

He would, too, he thought, knowing that in a moment she would open the door and close it behind her, and leave him here alone. He would like just to go for a drive with her one day, to wind down the windows, feel the thrum of the tyres on the motorway and know that she was there; the rare beauty of her, there beside him, if only for a while. It was more than he deserved. It was – it would be – enough.

For Della

The dogs were getting restless. Rosie was sitting beside the chair, a paw on Lizzy's lap; Jim was tracing slow circles around the kitchen. He wasn't as fast on his feet as he'd once been; there were grey hairs around his muzzle, and he slept for hours, day and night. Both dogs did, curled together on the big old bed under the radiator that was rancid with dried mud and dog-musk, but which Lizzy hadn't the heart to wash, for fear of removing what must surely also be the enduring traces of her mother's scent.

'All right,' she said, and Jim, at the door, lifted himself to his feet. Rosie, beside her, removed her paw. 'You win. We'll go out now.'

In the hallway Lizzy drew on her coat, hat, gloves and took the two leads from their hooks; she walked the dogs mostly off-lead, as the garden gate led straight out on to fields, but there was a section of road on the returning leg of her usual route. Her mother's route, really. Christine had walked it twice daily for ten years, in all weathers, with only minor variations – a short-cut through the thicket beside the church if she or either of the dogs was unwell, or the weather was particularly vile; a longer version for Sundays and holidays. Lizzy had joined her many times, wondering how her mother could bear to walk the same patch of earth so often, to trudge along the same, unchanging path. Once she'd said this aloud and Christine had replied, 'But it's always changing. Just look around you, Lizzy. It's never the same. Everything's always in a state of flux.' Lizzy hadn't really absorbed this at the time – had dismissed it, more or less, as part of her mother's general hippy-dippy philosophy – but it made sense to her now that she was the one walking the circuit twice a day. Or more usually once, if she was honest: she had work to keep up with, and the dogs were older now, they didn't need quite as much exercise as they once had.

They were still nippy, though; Rosie darted out as soon as Lizzy opened the back door, a slender greyhound blur arcing across the grass. Lizzy leant down to tickle the top of Rosie's head through her gloves; then she did the same to Jim, and together they went on, out of her mother's garden into the narrow, high-sided path that led to the first of the broad winter fields.

Her mother's garden. Her mother's house. Lizzy still thought of them both as such, though of course Christine was no longer here. Last will and testament, estate, probate: these were not terms that Lizzy could associate with her mother; she would not have been at all surprised if Christine had died without making a will. But no, she had seen to it all. She'd had a solicitor, an accountant, a financial adviser and of course her agent, Bel: a small cadre of people overseeing her business affairs, of which there'd been many, since *Fox in a Box* had done so well. The book, and its offspring – *Fox in Socks*, *Fox in Clocks*, and so on – had bought the cottage, too, and left more among Christine's various savings and investments (more words Lizzy struggled to imagine her mother using) than Lizzy could ever have imagined. She knew her mother had come into money, of course. The books had topped the bestseller charts for months, and Christine had shared a large chunk of their proceeds with her – the deposit for the house in Bristol; the car; a generous ISA. But they'd never really talked about the specifics of what Christine was worth: Lizzy because she considered this her mother's business, and her mother, Lizzy assumed, because on some level the fact that she had, quite suddenly and unexpectedly, become wealthy had embarrassed her, been almost a source of shame.

They were out in the open fields now; to Lizzy's right, a rolling expanse of bare brown earth; to her left, the greenish, wizened stumps of oilseed rape, with its bitter, boiled-turnip smell. The path carved a yellow stripe through the low wintering plants; the dogs loped on. The widescreen sky was off-white, grey in places, in others admitting jagged portions of blue; the weather wasn't bad, really, for the Sunday before Christmas. Lizzy undid the buttons of her coat. Astonishing, it still seemed to her, to have a whole swathe of southern England roll out before you and not spy another human soul: just farmhouses, and sky, and telegraph poles, and fields stretching out to the horizon like a rougher, greener version of the sea she'd grown up watching, as finely attuned to its moods and transformations as her mother had been to her own.

Yes, home, when Lizzy thought of it, was there, not here, not the house in Bristol, nor the others she'd lived in since university. The flat in Cliftonville, facing the Channel. Bought, Lizzy knew, because it was cheap – this had been a very long time before *Fox in a Box* – and because Christine had just finished her art degree, had found a job teaching at a school in Margate. The same one Lizzy had gone to ten years later, though her mum had no longer been teaching there; it wasn't as bad as it had been, but it was still a dump, as much of Margate had been in the mid-1990s, decades before the new gallery and the hipster cafés and the marauding London hordes. Lizzy wondered sometimes –

had done so quite often to her mother, aloud – whether her entire education, their entire *lives*, really, had been conducted on principle, as a kind of radical socialist experiment. But it hadn't done her any harm in the end; this had, in fact, usually been Christine's response. Lizzy had got on all right, had ended up at university. She even had a residual affection for her old school now, with its concrete and prefab classrooms and the metal detector that had been installed at the front gate when Lizzy was in Year 9, to screen arriving and departing pupils for concealed knives. 'Well,' Lizzy remembered her godmother, Della, saying deadpan at the time, 'nobody can say you're raising her in a bubble, can they, Christine?'

Della. Shit. What time were they due there again – one o'clock? Lizzy checked her watch: it was almost twelve; she'd slept in, no wonder the dogs had been climbing the walls. She'd better take the shortcut. At the far hedge she turned, choosing the path that led back in a tighter loop to the village, the church, the copse of trees. Called to the dogs to follow her, and they did, panting to catch up, the muscles in their haunches tightening and releasing as they overtook her and ran on.

They ate in the kitchen: the dining room was freezing in winter. The dogs sprawled before the range, two threadbare rugs, a smaller third, Picasso, Della's arthritic cat, lying between them, his head on Rosie's paw.

After lunch, Lizzy and Della went upstairs to the living room – the house, a converted oast, had an inverted layout, one of its many idiosyncrasies – while Robert took the dogs out; he'd been in the kitchen all morning cooking, and said he could use a breath of air. Lizzy knew that he was also beating a tactful retreat. The room was decorated for the season as only Della knew how: baubles hanging from bare, sculptural branches; a tarnished menorah (Robert's father had been Jewish) on the windowsill; tinsel strung between the paintings and prints that lined the walls, somehow managing to look stylish rather than tacky. Della lit the wood-burner, Picasso took up a new position before the fire and the women sat with their glasses of wine, watching the flames dance through the small blackened screen.

'What time do you want me on Christmas Day?'

Della was sitting straight-backed on a cushion on the floor, her legs curled under her. She still had that loose elegance, that dancer's poise, though she'd never been a dancer, not as far as Lizzy knew. 'Whenever suits,' she said. 'We'll probably eat about six. Come for a late breakfast, if you like.' She looked up at Lizzy, sitting a few feet away on the sofa, clutching a cushion to her chest. 'Are you really sure you don't want to come on Christmas Eve? We were thinking of going to midnight Mass.'

Lizzy shook her head. 'I want to wake up at Mum's, I think. Just be alone there for a bit, you know?'

Della watched her for a moment, then looked back at the fire. 'I do.'

They were silent for a while. There were many places Lizzy felt her mother's absence – her presence, it seemed to Lizzy now that she was gone, had extended everywhere, fallen across everything – but few, outside Christine's own cottage, spoke of it as loudly as Della and Robert's living room. The chair that had been Christine's – an old flea-market thing, reupholstered by Della in a bright Moroccan print – sat empty on the other side of the room, beneath the window. Lizzy didn't know whether Della and Robert sat in it when she wasn't here, but they never did so when she was, never. *Elijah's chair*: the phrase floated into

135

her mind as she sipped her wine, dredged from somewhere: a book, perhaps, or Robert, describing some aspect of family history and tradition. It was a Jewish ritual, wasn't it? The chair left empty, the prophet awaited.

Christine had adored Christmas; had made of it her own magpie festival, keeping the traditions she liked, dispensing with those she didn't, inventing others on a whim. When Lizzy was small, Christine had decided that Christmas Eve demanded a barbecue on the beach: sausages and baked potatoes, heated in the oven in their foil jackets and then finished on the portable stove Robert dragged down on to the sand. He and Della were in the downstairs flat then, Christine and Lizzy on the floors above; they'd been at art school together, Christine and Della, were closer to each other than either was to her own sister. Neighbours and friends had joined the party; there had been a bonfire, other children running around, wrapped up tightly in their coats and scarves. That was what Lizzy remembered most clearly about those nights: the flames rising, flaring yellow and orange against the black sky; the stars, the dark, impatient sea, all of it blurring together as she ran with the other kids, chasing and weaving, until she fell exhausted into her mother's arms. Sitting warm in her lap, twisting a lock of Christine's hair in her hand, listening to someone strum through stoned renditions of Christmas songs on his guitar. 'Jingle Bells'. 'Silent Night'. 'I Believe in Father Christmas'.

Lizzy had told all this to Lara, once. She had stared back at her, her eyes wide – they'd been in bed in the Bristol house, each lying on her side, drinking the other in. 'Wow. And there was I sitting with my mum and dad watching *Chitty Chitty Bang Bang*. She's something, your mum, isn't she?'

Yes. She was, she was. Sitting with her godmother now, neither of them speaking, both of them watching the wood burn.

Lizzy still hadn't found a present for Della. She'd ordered some gifts online – books, records, some handmade bits and pieces from Etsy – and trawled the streets of Lenbourne and Canterbury for other things, seeking out the smaller, independent shops. She'd bought a posh candle for Robert's sister Fran; Lizzy hadn't decided yet whether to go to her Christmas party, but if she did she couldn't turn up empty-handed. She'd dithered for ages over a set of chunky earthenware mugs for Jake – he'd said he was short on kitchen stuff for his caravan. But in the end she'd decided to leave them; she could tell he was nursing a bit of a thing for her and she didn't want to give him the wrong idea.

Della was tricky to buy for, had such a singular style. As a child, Lizzy had made all her gifts for Della, and not only because there was so little spare money to spend on Christmas, but because her godmother genuinely seemed to prefer the things Lizzy made with her own hands. A drawing, a painting; the year Lizzy was ten, a scrappy piece of music, performed on the piano Christine had recently found in a junk shop in Herne Bay. They had sat there on Christmas morning, listening to Lizzy play: Della, Robert and Christine, each in their finery (Christine insisted they all dress up for Christmas Day), nursing their hangovers from the previous night's party, which had gone on until the small hours, Lizzy falling asleep in her seafront bedroom to the strains of revelry below. The performance had been clumsy, the whole thing tortuous (she'd much rather just have bought her godmother some bath salts from Woolworths), but when she'd finished, Lizzy had swivelled on the piano stool and seen the three of them beaming at her, as if she'd just delivered a solo recital at the Albert Hall.

'Lizzy, that was wonderful!' Della said. 'You're a marvel. The best Christmas present ever.' And Lizzy had believed her, despite her own reservations; had floated through the rest of the day, giddy on her godmother's praise, thinking that perhaps she might become a composer or a virtuoso pianist, that she would sit down to practise for three hours a day until the notes fell like water from her hands.

The resolution hadn't lasted into the new year – in truth, Lizzy was no natural musician – but it was the way Della had made her feel that was the important thing. That sense that she could achieve anything she set her mind to – her mother had taught her this but Della had echoed it, deepened it, offered supporting evidence that it was true. For there they both were, her mother and her mother's best friend, two women who'd fled their families, dropped their suburban chains – Della's in Swansea, Christine's in Welwyn Garden City, which they visited infrequently, Lizzy's aunt and grandparents seeming hardly more interested in her than she and her mother were in them – and remade themselves in images of their own choosing. Christine a mother at twenty-two, made pregnant by a man whose identity she would never, as long as she lived, disclose. 'He's nothing,' she told Lizzy. 'He doesn't matter. He never did.' And Lizzy had believed this, too; had never spent much time wondering who or where her father was, other than to persuade herself that he had died, or never, despite the biological impossibility, existed at all.

Della had chosen never to have children. 'I have you, don't I?' she said frequently to Lizzy. 'You, and Robert, and your mother, and my work.' But both women had chosen art. Christine did illustration, her drawings intricate, detailed, ink-pen and water-colour wash. Della was moving from painting – bold, abstract portraits that had lined the walls of her studio in Margate, seeming to follow Lizzy with their bulbous, cyclopic eyes – to sculpture: installations, twisted wire and burnished sheets of metal that she worked herself with a blowtorch, masked and gloved like something out of *Flashdance*. Lizzy had watched Della sometimes after school, while her mother was teaching; sitting in a corner of the studio, her homework on her lap, music on the stereo – the Smiths, Kraftwerk, Depeche Mode – as her godmother worked, so absorbed in her task that an hour or more could pass before she lifted her visor and remembered that Lizzy was there.

As a child, Lizzy had been almost as accustomed to Della putting her to bed as to her mother doing so: they all moved easily between the two flats, up and down the stairs, keys held to both front doors. There was a thing, a hippy poem or incantation, that they said to her each night, Christine and Della, before closing the door and leaving her to sleep. *Good night little one. Sleep well. Know that you can do anything you set your mind to. Know that you are who you are meant to be.* She didn't know which of them had come up with it first, but that, until she was twelve or thirteen, had been the last thing Lizzy had heard before dropping off to sleep.

'Imagine,' she'd told Lara years later, 'being told every night that you can achieve anything, and then finding that you can't. That you're just not *special* enough.' For by then Lizzy had known that she would never be an artist, or a composer, or a pianist; she couldn't act, or dance, or excel at sport. She had a 2:1 in History from Bristol – an excellent university, sure; a tough, competitive course. But after a decade kicking her heels in various fields, from recruitment to marketing, she was a tutor, helping rich kids resit their exams: not exactly following her dreams.

After the split with Lara, Lizzy had seen a psychotherapist for a while (she never had quite decided what to call the woman – counsellor? therapist? shrink?). In her bright, book-cluttered consulting room in Redland, the woman had wondered aloud whether Lizzy had, in effect, been raised by two mothers, and now felt as if she had disappointed them both. This was after *Fox in a Box* had been published, become a sensation, a 'modern children's classic'. And Della had just been awarded a show at the Yorkshire Sculpture Park; there'd been extensive coverage, an interview with her in the *Sunday Times*. Lizzy, sitting opposite the psychotherapist, or whatever she called herself, on an uncomfortable hard-backed chair, had opened her mouth to refute this, and then found herself closing it again. 'Maybe you're right,' she'd said. 'Maybe I do feel like I've let them both down.'

Robert felt it too, Lizzy thought – differently, of course, but still, he felt it. He had never seemed quite solid to her, quite fully three-dimensional: liquid, diffident, the edges of him bleeding into the background. She didn't even really know what Robert did for a living – something to do with civil engineering, with bridges and railways; something that had, over the years, proved lucrative enough to buy the oast house and the land around it, which they'd done long before Della had started making any money with her art. At Della's fiftieth, which Lizzy had attended with Lara, she'd found herself standing next to Robert for a while in the marquee. The band playing; Lara off somewhere; Della and Christine dancing together to The Cure in the middle of the throng; Robert, gently drunk, putting his arm around her and saying, 'Dear Lizzy. Little Lizzy. Not easy for us, is it, living always in their shadow?'

Was that, Lizzy thought now, sitting with her laptop on her mother's bed – she had taken, in the weeks after the funeral, to sleeping there: it was the biggest, nicest room in the cottage, and still painfully, joyfully filled with her mother's clothes and books and lotions and perfume – what she was doing here? Living in her mother's cottage eighteen months since her death. The Bristol house rented, her own life abandoned, hardly a thing of her mother's touched or sold or dealt with in any meaningful way since she had come to be with Christine at the end and never left. It was pathetic, really, Lizzy thought, scrolling aimlessly through gift options for Della online. It was just as Lara, ever the physicist, had said to her at the end: she was like Newton's first law of motion, never taking action, never diverting course unless that action was forced upon her. 'It's exhausting, Lizzy,' Lara had said when she'd left. 'You want me to make all the decisions. It's like you want me to live your life for you. Well, I can't do it any more. It's too much pressure.'

No, it was no good; she could see nothing that was right for Della. She'd be better turning up at the oast for Christmas with a bottle of wine and a lump of coal. Lizzy closed the laptop, set it down on the carpet; lay down on her side, still fully dressed, and drew the duvet up over her. There was silence, for a while – deep country silence, unmarred by patrol cars or passers-by – and then the patter and creak of two elderly dogs making their way up onto the bed from the floor. Two warm bodies, nestling into hers, following her into stillness.

The next few days were fine and cold; wide pink skies in the morning, frost shattering beneath her boots as she crossed the fields with the dogs. Real winter weather that even the hardy oil-fired boiler couldn't quite cope with; Lizzy understood now, deep into her second winter in the cottage, why her mother had felt the cold so much after moving here. She thought of

Jake in his caravan; he only had an electric heater, said he slept under two duvets on the coldest nights. 'You should get a dog,' she'd told him. 'Best way to keep warm.' And then regretted the implication that there might have been other, more intimate ways. But he'd only nodded and said, 'Yeah. Maybe I should.'

She saw Jake at the Parachute Christmas party; he looked well, better than she'd ever seen him, really. A clean, pressed shirt, his hair washed, and something different, she thought, in the way he carried himself; she was more aware of his height, and she realised that he'd lost that slight stoop common to tall, unhappy men. By the end of the night, she knew why; he invited her outside, said he had something to show her. She shrugged on her coat, followed him into the darkness – worried, just for a second, that she might have made a mistake: how well, after all, did she really know him? But the anxiety was fleeting; he only wanted to show her his new car, a gift, he said, from a mechanic, his oldest friend. Lizzy admired it; they climbed inside and it came over her again – the knowledge, instinctive, unspoken, of what Jake felt for her. She could sense it, as clearly as if he'd opened his mouth and confessed. Gently, then, Lizzy did the speaking for him, offered him the truth – which was, she had lived long enough to know, the greater kindness. They sat in silence, and she sensed the slow, deliberate recalibration of his assumptions.

'I really like talking to you, Lizzy,' Jake had said eventually, his voice brave and bright. 'Maybe we could just hang out a bit outside the meetings, go out somewhere in the car. A walk by the sea, like. Whitstable or Folkestone. It's nice there these days. Posh. As friends. You know what I mean?'

'I do know,' Lizzie had said, and meant it. 'I'd like that, Jake.'

Later that night, as Patricia drove her home (she'd been in AA for twenty years), Lizzy felt a new lightness come over her, a sense of release. The feeling continued into the following day; she woke early, went out with the dogs while the garden was still in darkness, watched the red dawn come up over the farmhouses on the far horizon. It wasn't really about Jake, she thought, with a fresh, startling clarity, one which seemed connected with the sharp, clear lines of the landscape around her, uncovered by the pale light: the naked trees, the bare hedgerows, the long, sweeping ridges of dark earth. She had felt badly for Jake, for his misplaced interest, but he wasn't the first man to have expressed feelings for her, and Lizzy had never considered it her responsibility to soothe anyone's shattered hopes. She was who she was, who she had always been, and this demanded no forewarning, no apology. Her mother had taught her this – her mother and Della. *Know that you are who you are meant to be.* The words washed over her anew; Lizzy could almost hear her mother speaking, and joy rose in her, a great giddying rush. She threw her arms wide and ran along the path – an aeroplane, wheeling and stumbling, Jim and Rosie cantering alongside her, barking, matching her exuberance with their own.

Back at the cottage, Lizzy showered, turning up the water as hot as she could bear. Dressed, fed the dogs, watched them flop, exhausted, on to their shared bed. The joy was still there, still with her, and she wanted to spread it; in her mother's bedroom – *her* bedroom, at least for now, perhaps forever – she took up her phone, texted friends in Bristol, London, Manchester, Berlin. *Happy Christmas. A few days early, I know, but I'm feeling the love right now. I'm Scrooge on Christmas morning. The clouds clearing. Love and miss you all xxx.*

There were carols on the radio, still tuned to Christine's favoured station – Lizzy left them on, reached under the bed for the suitcase her mother had always kept there, as she had back in the flat in Cliftonville, a battered old red-plastic thing from the 1980s, dusty and cracked. Lined up the numbers on the dial – the month and year of Lizzy's birth – and laid the case open on the bed. Postcards, photographs, yellowing ticket stubs from decades-old concerts, plays, exhibitions: her mother had been sentimental like that. There were stacks of boxes in the attic, though Christine had cleared some of them in the move from Margate – piles of Lizzy's old schoolbooks and folders, lined with her careful, looping, childish hand. Here was one now – *Elizabeth Cooper, Class 4B*. She'd look at this later, and the rest of it, unopened since her mother's death. Her quarry was elsewhere, among the glossy Kodak snaps printed from real film, the black reels sent off in sealed bags, their processed memories returned a week or so later, landing fatly on the mat downstairs in the communal hall.

They had pored over them together, Christine and Lizzy, sitting at the kitchen table, the gulls wheeling and calling outside. Lizzy in her yellow anorak and red wellies on a walk at Dungeness, bright splashes of colour against the brown shingle. Della and Robert on Minnis Bay in summertime, the clouds high and hazy in Turner's blurred watercolour sky. Della and Christine on the sofa, heads close together, sharing some private confidence. And further back, to before Lizzy was born: Della and Christine at art school, at parties, waving cigarettes and glasses of red wine. Then the four of them – their strange, lopsided family – shown in various combinations, places, styles. Robert and Lizzy. Della and Lizzy. Christine and Robert. Robert and Della. Della, Lizzy and Christine.

Here it was, right at the bottom, typically; the bed was strewn with photographs now, the suitcase almost empty. But this was it. Round-cornered, slightly overexposed; they were all a little bleached, sun-dazzled. Well, not Lizzy; her eyes were closed, she was swaddled in a white blanket, hours old. A hospital bed.

Christine lying against white pillows, her hair plastered to her head, a triumphant warrior queen. Della holding Lizzy, looking up at the photographer – a nurse, perhaps; this was, Lizzy knew, before Robert had been on the scene – lifting the baby slightly, as if in offering. An aunt, an older sister, a godmother, presenting the newborn to some tribal elder, unseen, beyond the lens.

Lizzy would frame the photograph – she would go into Lenbourne that afternoon and buy a frame. She would wrap it and give it to Della on Christmas Day as her own small tribute, her own offering to the woman who had helped to raise her, and for whom she needed – Lizzy knew this now, bone-deep, a blade slicing through the layers of grief and loss and sadness, the ideas about what her life was, and was not, and should have been – to be nothing, no one, other than who and what she was.

For Robert

He was standing beside the door, framed against the dawn. She watched what he was watching: the broad, heavy-bellied sky, the fierce flames of light at the horizon, which would shortly rise, leaching their colours into the clear, pure light of day.

'Here,' Della said, and Robert turned, took the mug. Black, double shot, a teaspoon of sugar. He was pale-skinned in his pyjamas, his navy towelling dressing gown with its loosening threads at the sleeve. His hair still thick, but now entirely grey.

They both woke early these days, Della naturally – she'd always been an early riser, didn't seem to need as much sleep as most people – and Robert out of necessity. He'd used to sleep so deeply – sometimes, at weekends, right into the middle of the morning, making up for his week of early commutes – but his sleep was fitful now; she often heard him moving around in the night. Sometimes, when she rose at six, Della found him in the living room, snoring, his head thrown back against the sofa, his neck painfully cricked; he'd be rubbing it later, hunting for ibuprofen.

Robert sipped his coffee and said, 'I'm worried about Lizzy.'

Della nodded. She pressed the button on the machine and it whirred and spluttered. 'I am too.'

'She just seems so . . . Lost. Unmoored.'

'She does. We all have been, I suppose, but Lizzy . . . of course it was going to hit her hard. But I thought she'd have sold the cottage by now. I think Christine would have wanted her to sell it and move on. Live her own life. She knows we'd take the dogs.'

Della sat; Robert remained standing. The day was coming on, shafts of greyish light slanting in through the broad expanses of glass. It had been open to the elements, this portion of the house, when they'd first bought the oast: a kind of covered terrace or veranda where the grain had once been unloaded; there were two square kilns where the hops had been heated and dried and a central, rectangular section their surveyor had called the 'granary'. Robert had taken a deep professional interest in all this, admiring the workmanship, the small feats of Victorian industrial engineering. But Della knew he was pained by the house's slow decay – there had been historic movement, the roofline of the granary sagged, there were cracks inside and out. The kitchen conversion had been Robert's idea: knocking through walls, remodelling the space, sealing in the veranda with glass.

'And she won't come on Christmas Eve? Spend the evening with us, wake up here?'

Della shook her head. 'She says she'll drive over in the morning.'

'Shame.'

Robert sat, frowning. She knew he was thinking about Christmas, which mattered to him far more than it ever had to her. His father Abe was the same, had embraced the pseudo-Christian festival with all the fervour of a new convert. Robert's grandparents had always kept Hanukah, and never quite forgiven Abe for marrying Robert's mother Katherine, a Catholic, lapsed as she was; though Katherine had brought the menorah

148

out each year. They had it now, had rescued it from among the vanloads of stuff Robert and Fran had disposed of when Abe went into The Oaks; it was upstairs in the living room, offering the comfort of its candles each night to the sheep in the neighbouring field.

'It's not the same without her, is it?' he said. 'I don't suppose it will ever be.'

Christine, he meant, of course; they had spent almost every Christmas together, the four of them – give or take the odd set of parents, relatives, waifs and strays – since the mid-1980s, for almost as long as Della and Robert had been together. Thirty-six years: an extraordinary length of time, though Della and Christine had known each other longer. Forty-one years they'd been friends, when Christine died. The previous year, they'd bought each other silver bracelets, threaded with red semi-precious stones; their friendship, they'd decided, deserved just as much celebration as any marriage, especially, Christine had joked, as neither of them had ever actually been a bride.

Della was still wearing her bracelet now – she never took it off, not even in the shower. She looked down at it, fine and delicate on her right wrist. She wondered where Christine's had gone, whether Lizzy had it now. She'd never seen Lizzy wearing it, but perhaps she'd consider that strange.

'No,' Della said. 'It won't be. Nothing will.'

Della was working on a piece for Robert: a Christmas present, though it wouldn't be ready for some weeks. She'd wanted to have it done sooner, unveil it on Christmas Day, remove the protective sheet with a magician's flourish (Della had an appetite for such moments of drama), but she'd struggled more than she'd expected with the clay maquettes, and now the foundry was closed until the new year.

They'd sent back the wax casting, anyway; she had it here in the studio, under a cloth veil. Robert had been issued with strict instructions not to enter without warning. She planned to bring him out here on Christmas morning, to at least show him this, her waxen prototype – though of course the sculpture looked nothing like it would when it was cast in bronze and set in the garden, tall and broad and solid, with a circular portion missing from the middle, like a window, a porthole, admitting the grass and sky beyond. She was retaining the missing portion, also casting it, and planning to set it a few feet away, on the ground, as if a section of the larger piece had simply wrested itself free and rolled off. In her mind she was calling it *Together, Apart*, though it wouldn't really need a formal title; she wouldn't want it ever to be sold, not in her lifetime. After that, Robert could do with it what he liked.

The idea had come to Della during the weeks Christine had spent in hospital. Terrible weeks, lost weeks; days blurring into night and night into day, time suspended, elastic, now speeding past, now ponderously slow. They had not been able to visit; only Lizzy had been permitted, pending negative tests, wearing scrubs and a visor and a mask, all the equipment that had been so culpably lacking in the beginning, but that still, Della feared, gave its wearers only an illusion of control. The inability to visit Christine, to be with her in her suffering, had been almost more than Della could bear: she'd been frantic, pacing the house and garden, howling at the moon (or, more often, at Robert). Most evenings, Lizzy drove over from the hospital; sat at the kitchen table, the night high and still beyond the glass, drinking their wine, offering snatches of information that Della absorbed like rare missives from another, distant world. The day Christine died they had sat there again, the three of them, for hours; drunk, by the end of it, horribly drunk, sad and angry and sobbing, stumbling to bed just before dawn, each of them falling into a separate blackening sleep.

Della had seen it clearly that night, this idea that had been hovering in the corners of her mind: two sculptures, placed close together, one a perfect circle, drawn from the belly of the other. This was how it worked for her, the genesis, the source: an image, fuzzy and indistinct, appeared (she didn't know where from: did anyone?) and began, over weeks, sometimes months, to assume solid, three-dimensional form. It was only then, once the image was developed, settled – once the real physical labour of manufacture had begun – that Della could begin to assign some meaning to it, to work out what she might, with this work, be trying to say. In the old days, she'd scorned such retrospective thinking: 'prettifying', she'd called it, insisting on art for art's sake, form over function, the artist's biography, even their intentions, irrelevant. She'd seen it as a way of belittling women in particular, of ensuring that they remained excluded from the grown-ups' table, the place where the real artists – almost always men – made art that was allowed to speak for itself. But Della had, in this as in so many other ways, softened over time; the gallerists, critics, interviewers demanded such things. Everybody needed a story.

What, then, was the story here? Their story – hers and Robert's – and hers and Christine's, too. One too complex, too multifaceted, to reduce to easy statements, pat phrases turned worn and familiar by repetition. *Well, with this piece, I was thinking about . . . You see, at this time in my life, I was . . .* No; this sculpture would not be subjected to such dissection. It would remain private, between the two of them, and them alone.

Few people knew the real story of how Della and Robert had met. They had the facts – a blind date, a first meeting so cringeworthy, so fundamentally unlikely, knowing Della, that it was trotted out often as a source of laughter, of knowing self-deprecation. *We were set up. I walked into the pub, and there he was* . . . But the mechanics of their meeting had remained deliberately obscure.

This was because it was actually Della's mother who had introduced them. Her mother, yes – Carys Evans, back in Swansea, in the three-bedroom semi with the three-piece suite and the rash of gnomes lining the weedless path to the front door. Carys Evans, whose boldest act had been to choose a name for her younger daughter on a whim, because she liked the sound of it, the music it made on her tongue.

Della was unapologetically snobbish about her mother, about every aspect of her origins; she'd felt different from them all for as long as she could remember, had believed herself destined for something, somewhere else – a conviction Carys had actively encouraged, fussing over her in a way she never really had with her elder daughter, Bethan. Della understood now, with the distance of time and maturity – and Bethan's sullen insistence – that Carys had suffered after Bethan's birth, that there had almost certainly been a period of undiagnosed postnatal depression. With Della, things had been different; their mother had, Bethan believed, been making up for what had gone wrong the first time. 'You got everything you wanted,' Bethan had told her frequently, before Della had stopped calling, before she'd allowed herself to pretend that she'd never had a sister, that Christine was the only sister she could ever need.

'Everything was so easy for you. She told *you* you could do anything, be anyone. That's not how it was with me.'

Carys, then, against all possible expectations, had been the architect of it all. Della was twenty-eight, living in Margate, having abandoned her secretarial course in London for art college in Canterbury. That was done, now – she had graduated, done her master's, was living in a flat in Cliftonville, in a tall, crumbling house that faced the sea. Christine was upstairs, with her daughter Lizzy, now almost two; she'd got pregnant unexpectedly, after a one-time thing at a party. Della had vowed to be there for them, to help, almost as if she'd been the guy Christine had hooked up with without even knowing his name – nor, of course, his phone number or address.

Neither of them had a boyfriend, much less a husband. Christine said she wasn't interested, her energies were all for Lizzy and the work she was doing when her daughter was asleep – intricate illustrations, ink and watercolour; she was thinking of making a series of children's books. Della was painting – big, abstract daubs that she feared were meaningless, second-rate – and helping to look after Lizzy, and having her own casual encounters now and then, but nothing that stuck. She told herself she didn't care, that this was freedom; but Carys was appalled, told her frequently on the phone that she was in danger of getting left on the shelf. What a phrase! Della laughed at her mother, told her how ridiculous she was, how provincial and small-minded. But if she were truly honest – which she rarely was, back then, with anyone, especially herself – the same worries dogged her, tugged at her sleeve. She was lonely, in truth; she loved Christine and Lizzy, but they were their own little unit, mother and child, and however close Della was to them, neither was truly hers.

So when her mother told her, one day, that there was

someone she really thought Della ought to meet – the son of a friend's friend from the Rotary Club, now making a big name for himself, and a salary to match, in London; working, Carys thought, as some kind of engineer – Della dismissed her, said she didn't need a blind date, of all things. But the idea was sown, and germinated, and a few weeks later she'd walked into the pub on Charlotte Street, scanning heads and faces for that of a man named Robert Samuels, who would, she had been told, be sitting at the bar, reading that day's copy of the *Guardian*. (Had it been the *Telegraph*, Della knew she would never have gone.) A man in a suit, standing rather than sitting, holding his newspaper in front of him like a shield. 'Robert?' she'd said, and he'd lowered it, and there he'd been: not tall, not short; neither particularly handsome, nor the opposite. Unremarkable, she'd thought, in every way; she'd almost turned and walked out, but then he'd smiled and offered to buy her a drink, and so she'd stayed, because she was thirsty, and she'd come all the way to London on the train so she might as well stick around to see what happened.

What happened was this. Robert bought her a sweet sherry (ordered as a joke, Della thinking of her mother, her Christmas thimbleful of Bristol Cream). She drank it in two swift gulps; he finished his pint. She bought a bottle of French plonk, asked for two glasses, found a table near the back of the pub. The bottle, perhaps, was the deciding factor; Della's eye was no longer on the door. She liked him – he might be wearing a suit, he might look more like an insurance salesman than the rough-hewn, leather-jacketed types she usually went for – but that was the truth of it: she liked him. He was only a few years older – thirty – but his manners were quaint, old-fashioned; he held the door open for her when they left the pub, insisted on walking with her to the station. They parted at the bottom of the escalator;

Robert was taking the Northern line, heading south (he lived in Clapham). Her destination was Victoria, and Kent. He told her what a great time he'd had, that he'd like to see her again, that he'd call; he had her number, her mother had passed it on. Della was non-committal. *Maybe, yeah, let's see.* Robert looked at her for a long moment before kissing her on the cheek and going on his way. She watched his departing back as it was swallowed by the crowd.

Later, on the train to Margate, even as Della told herself that the evening had been a waste of time, that she wasn't interested in Robert Samuels at all, she watched her shadowy reflection in the window, wondering what he'd thought of her, whether he'd found her attractive; wondering how long it would be until he called, and what she would say to him when he did.

The supermarket was busy: there were only two days to go until Christmas Eve.

'Remind me why we didn't order online again, Robert?' Della said as they retrieved a trolley from the chain beside the door.

'Because, my love' – he was sorting the bags – 'we like to see what we're buying, don't we? Especially at Christmas. It's not the same, getting it all delivered.'

Della thought it was far worse, but did not say so aloud. She knew he enjoyed it all – the music, the decorations, the supermarket workers wearing reindeer antlers and tinsel boas, even the crowds of shoppers, who were mostly good-natured, seasonally smiling – smiles you could actually see, now that so many people were no longer bothering with masks. Della had burnt all of hers – actually burnt them, cast them witch-like, gleeful, on to one of Robert's midsummer bonfires. (That appetite for drama again.) Robert still had his, he still wore it quite often, said he didn't want to tempt fate; normality, they all knew now, was too fragile a concept to take for granted.

Della sighed; she hated food-shopping at the best of times. 'Can we start at the other end, with the wine? Work our way back?'

The look Robert gave her was pained; he had a system, especially at Christmas. Start with the fruit and veg, then move round logically, aisle by aisle. Avoid the buy-one-get-one-free offers and anything that had flown too far. He had his list with him, and a pen to tick off each item as they placed it in the bags. The list was in his hand now. He looked down; following his gaze, Della scanned the first few lines. *Parsnips. Potatoes. Brussels sprouts.*

'Oh, all right,' she said. 'As we were.'

Music rattled from ceiling speakers: the Pretenders, '2000 Miles'. One of Robert's favourites. She was pushing the trolley; he was by the potatoes, waiting politely for a woman in a Father Christmas jumper to step out of his way – the vegetable section was rammed, everyone everywhere, for one portion of the year, wanting to buy exactly the same thing. She watched him lean down, examine the boxes of potatoes in their plastic sacks. He straightened, turned. 'King Edwards or Maris Pipers?'

She smiled. There was comfort in this, wasn't there: the yearly ritual, the choosing, the preparing, the cooking; the running smoothly along the usual, expected grooves, whatever chaos and confusion the year had brought. 'We like the King Edwards, don't we? Better for roasting.'

He returned her smile; boyish suddenly, happy, she knew, in the simplicity of the decision, of this small, shared choice. 'Yes. King Edwards it is.'

They roamed the aisles; the trolley filled up, until pushing it became a strain. Robert took over, handed her the list. 'Here. Christmas pudding next. And mince pies. You're not still thinking of making any, are you?'

Della shook her head. They had taken to baking them together, she and Christine, finding a free December afternoon, putting on their aprons and covering the kitchen – the oast's, usually; it was bigger, the range superior – in flour and smears of jarred mincemeat. It was a game, really, a kind of playtime, assuming the role both of them had avoided in their real lives: the country wife, brisk and capable, ruling her domestic empire. Christine had cooked, of course – there had been no one else to do it for her – but only from necessity, with no real pleasure. Della also made meals when she had to, but with a similar indifference. The oast kitchen was Robert's domain; he was a wonderful cook and it was, they agreed, the primary outlet for his creativity. His work had been creative once, perhaps – the bridges, the roads, the big civil projects – there had been beauty in these, but age and success had carried him further from the work he loved into strategy, management, consultancy. It depressed him, Della knew, it depressed her, too. But what was there to do? In a few years, Robert would retire and then he could do what he liked. Cook, she supposed; and garden; and potter around the house in his slippers like the old man he was.

They had never married, never had children. Most assumed these had been Della's choices, but this was not so: she had asked Robert to marry her several times, the first of these just months after they'd met, when they were in bed together in the flat in Cliftonville.

It was the middle of the day, a Saturday; they could hear Lizzy running around upstairs (it was extraordinary how much noise a toddler could produce on bare boards). They had been in bed since the previous evening, when Della had met Robert from the London train; she'd gone out for fish and chips, brought them back to bed, and the sheets were now faintly rank with salt and vinegar and chip-grease. Robert was astonishing in bed; there was so much about him that she hadn't expected. He knew his music – the more alternative, the better; some of the bands he loved she'd never come across, not even at art school – and he had a talent for poker, attended a weekly game. Her early barricades had been demolished. Della was hooked, obsessed, hardly able to paint, late for her shifts at the café, unable to think about anything but him, and them, and this: the two of them together, unclothed, undressing for each other, too, the shapes and mysteries of their respective pasts.

'We should get married, shouldn't we?' she said. 'Have a big white wedding. A meringue. Pageboys. Everything. My mother would be beside herself.'

They were lying on their backs, watching the ceiling, their legs entwined. She felt his body shift and resettle as she spoke. The silence that followed was long and strained, filled with the footsteps of the stampeding elephant upstairs. Della was determined not to break it; she withdrew her leg from his, lay motionless beside him. Eventually, Robert said, 'It is amazing, this thing, Della, it really is. But you need to know this: I don't want to get married and I don't want to have children. Not with you, not with anyone. I really don't, and I won't. I need you to understand that, to really understand. I won't ever change my mind.'

This had not, Della knew, landed as quite the revelation it should have been; she had actually laughed, shifted on to her front, placed her arm across his chest. 'Silly man. For God's sake, who's talking about children? I was only joking, anyway.'

She was twenty-eight years old, and she had Lizzy, had her work; she wasn't absolutely sure she wanted children, and the marriage idea had been a whim. Months passed. Robert moved in with her, let his flat, commuted to London. Della found studio space in an abandoned warehouse, her work deepened and matured; there were exhibitions, a few sales, she was able to quit her job at the café (there was Robert's money, too; he insisted on covering the mortgage, and her peppercorn studio rent). It was when Della turned thirty – a dreadful cliché, she supposed, but there it was, even the most banal things could be true – that the thoughts returned to her; thoughts she had not expected, not chosen, but that floated through her mind of their own volition. A wedding: a public commitment, a party, a pair of fine gold rings. Children, shadowy and nameless – the idea of children, really, not their messy, demanding reality. Lizzy was almost five now, and about to start school; she was wonderful, surprising, her own small, determined being, but she wasn't Della's own.

She asked him again – *let's get married, let's think about kids* – and his reaction astounded her. Robert was furious, angrier than she'd ever seen him; he actually shouted, slammed the door, and went off to spend the night in a hotel. (She wondered now, with the distance of time and experience, whether a good deal of his anger had sprung from guilt, or at least fear – the fear that he was denying her too much, that he might lose her.) That night, Della barely slept; in the morning, still early, she called her mother, sure of the advice she would be offered. *Leave him. Walk away. He's not serious about you. Call it off.* Della was, after all, still on the proverbial shelf. Her mother loved Robert, told everyone she knew that she'd solved the problem of her

159

daughter's singledom herself; but at this, surely, Carys would draw the line.

But Carys, too, had surprised her. She was just up, smoking her first cigarette; Della could picture her, there in the Swansea kitchen, with its fitted pine units and tiles printed with pictures of wicker baskets and bread loaves. Carys listened, and after a lengthy pause she spoke, in that lovely sing-song voice Della had realised, in that moment, she missed; she had lost her own Welsh accent, softened it, at first deliberately, then without noticing, with all the time she'd spent away – as far as she could get, really, without falling off the land mass of their shared island.

'Della,' her mother said. 'Children are wonderful. You know I love you and Bethan more than anything. But they're not the only thing. One day, they leave, and then it's just the two of you. Is Robert the man you want to be with then? If so, think very carefully. Don't just throw that away. And anyway' – she drew deeply on her Benson & Hedges – 'you have your art, don't you? It's going well, and it's important to you. Are you sure there's room to be a wife and mother, too?'

Robert stayed in the hotel for three nights. When he returned, they were both chastened; for weeks they were solicitous with one another, extravagantly kind. The argument slipped off into the past, and it was only over time – weeks and months, summer shifting into autumn and onwards into winter, which was cold that year: angry, gusting winds, testy, whipping sea – that Della realised her decision had been made. And she did not regret it – not often, not in any serious way. For this was what she had, what she had chosen – this man, this home, this life. And if she wondered, sometimes, about the children there might have been had Robert felt differently – saw the shapes of their faces, sometimes, in her dreams – it was only briefly, their images as vague and transient as shadowy reflections in old foxed glass.

There was wine still to buy, and spirits, and a few more gifts: something for the cleaner, Ilona; something for Les, the postman, who always left their parcels at the front door, even when they weren't in; something for Eddy at Valley Motors, who serviced the car, had saved them so much money and hassle over the years.

Booze, too, for Fran and Adam's party. Gin, and cognac, and tequila for Lizzy, who loved a margarita, though they didn't know yet whether she was coming with them; all of it went into the trolley and the bags, now stacked on top of one another, so full that Della feared the uppermost bottles might slide off and crash on to the floor.

'Here,' Robert said, 'let me rearrange things.' Della let him – neither would dispute that he was the more practical of the two – and took her phone from her bag. A missed call from Lizzy, and a message. Della opened it, and a smile crept across her face.

'Who's that?' said Robert.

'Lizzy. She tried to call just now. Then sent a message. Listen. *Dearest D, just tried to ring – is it today you're doing the big shop? I'd have come and helped if so. Just wanted to tell you that something's shifted for me – I don't know what it is exactly, but I'm feeling so much better. Happier. More productive. Like Radiohead – ha! (Ask Robert what that means.) Just wanted to let you know this. Maybe I will come on Christmas Eve after all, if that's OK with you both? I might even make it to Fran's party. Much love. Call me when you're done.'*

They stared at each other across the loaded trolley.

'Radiohead?' Della said. 'What does she mean?'

Robert was grinning. 'It's from a song. "Fitter Happier". One of their best.'

'That's wonderful then, isn't it? That she's feeling better?'

'It is,' he said, and he leant over, kissed her. 'It really is.'

That night, after Robert had gone to bed – he was tired, had slept poorly again – Della went out to her studio.

The night was black and icy; there was so little light pollution out here, though they could hear the thrum of the motorway when the wind blew towards the house, and the sky was filled with stars. The deep darkness of the lane beyond the gravel drive still frightened her. Pathetic, really, childish, but even childish fears had their origins. Della hurried on; the studio was unlocked and she'd left the electric heater plugged in, knowing she might return.

Robert's sculpture – its wax version, at least – stood in the middle of the huge, high-ceilinged room; the building had once been a barn, they assumed this had been where they'd kept the sacks of hops, or maybe the horses and their carts. Now it was where she worked: her space, familiar, everything exactly where she wanted it. A room of her own. She was lucky, in this and in so many ways. She stood for a moment, taking in the form of the sculpture under its sheet; there was work still to be done, just a few finishing touches, she'd take a few hours the following day, before Fran's party. For now, it was enough to stand here and know that it existed, this thing she had made – for Robert, for herself, for the life they shared.

For Fran

There were far worse places than The Oaks; Robert tried to remind himself of that each time he visited.

The main building was tall, broad, rather elegant, with high windows set in convex bow fronts: Georgian or early Victorian, more like a seafront town house than a nursing home on an unlovely stretch of the Canterbury Road. It had been built as a private house, owned, Robert imagined, by one of the old Jackson's brewery grandees: he pictured a man with a pocket watch, a woman sewing in a morning room; tea on the lawn, white dresses, games of tennis. There had once been a grass court, though this, as with most of the land behind the home, had been requisitioned by the large red-brick extension. The walled garden, at least, had been retained, with its low-hedged borders and a pond that some health and safety manager had, in their wisdom, decided to surround with a wire fence.

The oak trees had been kept, too – there was one in front of his father's window, which overlooked the road. Through most of the year, Abe's view was of the tree's generous green spread, flaming to yellows and golds in the autumn; it was only now, in winter, that the tree stood bare, its fretwork of branches stamped against the grey sky, admitting glimpses of the sad little parade of shops across the street. A fish and chip place – *Tuesday special: buy one cod get one free* – and a dusty newsagent, the shelves in its window mostly empty, a wire-caged board outside displaying the latest headlines from the *Lenbourne Gazette*: 'Oh no, it isn't': *your panto season guide*.

Abe was in his armchair – wingback, beige wipeable plastic, with a tray that folded down across his lap. His head was thrown back against the antimacassar, his eyes glued shut. Behind him, on the sideboard, one of the few pieces they'd been able to bring with him from Cardiff, someone – Fran, Robert assumed – had arranged his Christmas cards in front of the family photographs, the age-spotted silver frames that had always, when they were children, sat on the corner bookcase in the lounge. There was the card Robert had brought a few weeks before – a Picasso dove, sweeping black lines on a white background, hardly what Robert would call festive, but the design had been Della's choice; she was the one who wrote them, after all. Another from Fran, Adam and the boys – a pair of penguins, a red bauble dangling from their conjoined beaks. One from the staff – the picture was of last year's Christmas tree, twelve feet high, positioned next to the central stairwell in the entrance hall, which was large and galleried, panelled with dark wood; if you ignored the plastic-covered noticeboard, the stairlift and support rails, you could almost imagine yourself in the atrium of a Scots baronial hotel. And so it should be, really; his father's residency here brought a price tag that Robert could still not quite comprehend, even though he'd been paying it for years – well, he and Fran, splitting the monthly bill between them, their parents' bungalow sold, all of that money gone, swallowed up by Abe's long illness, his infinitely slow decline. His father was dying, it seemed to Robert in his darker moments, as he had lived: quietly, with minimal fuss, but without much evident volition either; not raging, not going gently, just existing, until eventually, they must all assume (the thought brought Robert both fear and relief), he would not.

His father was vulnerable in repose; his neck, exposed, was greyish, wrinkled, and seemed naked somehow, like a tortoise's, soft above its hard shell. Nothing about Abe, though, was, or had ever been, hard; he was all softness and give, it was Robert's mother Katherine who'd been all rigidity. Abe had loved her once; his father's one major act of will, it seemed to Robert, had been to defy his family and marry her. Perhaps that had used up all his energy. An unhappy marriage: that was all, in the end, it had been. An ancient, familiar story. And yet it broke Robert, a little, to look at his father, sitting there with his head slumped back against the chair, and think of how different things might have been for him, for his mother, for them all, if Abe had only had the courage to confront what was happening and make a change. But perhaps Abe had believed that there was nothing amiss in this, in his wife's dissatisfaction, the arguments and silences, the sour, pursed expression she wore in his presence, as if in perpetual anticipation of disappointment. Perhaps, until the end, he had simply loved her.

It was after twelve; Robert should be getting back, Lizzy was coming for lunch. It pained Robert to think of Abe waking alone in the room; or perhaps he wouldn't notice, it was hard to know what his father did notice these days, and there was his routine to comfort him, the institutionalised timetable of meals, activities, television. Roast beef today; Robert could smell it, wafting up from the basement kitchen, with the inevitable accompanying whiff of boiled cabbage. Why *did* these places always smell of boiled cabbage, whether cabbage was being boiled or not?

Robert crossed the room, stood for a moment beside his father's chair, not wanting to wake him, not wanting to leave without saying goodbye. 'Bye Dad,' he said quietly, pressing his fingers briefly to the loose crêpe-paper sag of his father's cheek. 'I'll be back in a few days, all right? Take care.'

Robert loved his train journeys in and out of London with a devotion that even he could see was out of all proportion. It wasn't the trains themselves – who could love a grubby, irregular commuter service? – or even the view, which was lovely in places, wide sky and flat, gunmetal estuary and sweeping fields, but mainly unremarkable, punctuated by new-build cul-de-sacs and industrial estates and the high tethered struts of the Dartford Crossing. Robert wasn't the type of traveller who insisted on the same seat every morning, who fell into a silent huff if that seat was taken. He was happy to move around, to change positions and carriages; occasionally, if the train was particularly busy, to stand. No, what Robert loved was the time the journey took, that blameless gift of rest; an hour and a quarter each way, give or take the odd delay, snatched from the regulated grid of his day.

He never worked on the train, tried not to check his email; he read, listened to music or podcasts on his headphones (there was a great American one from NPR, discussing new albums every Friday), or more often just sat and stared out the window, letting his thoughts roll in time with the train's onward gait. It was the pace he liked; Robert enjoyed driving, too, but there was something particular about this measured, rhythmic speed, something that perhaps took him back to childhood, to the journeys they had taken east to see their Samuels grandparents. Cardiff to London; their mother silent for once, absorbed in *Good Housekeeping*, their father smoothing out the *Telegraph*. Robert playing games with Fran – snap, travel tiddlywinks, draughts; anything as long as she kept quiet, as long as she didn't disturb their mother's peace. The familiar refrains of those years, still echoing in the memory. *Keep it down, I'm resting. Play nicely, can't you? Not now, I'm not feeling well. I'm busy. I'm tired. For God's sake – can't you ever, for one minute, leave me in peace?*

The train was just coming into London, approaching Bromley South, when Robert's phone rang. He had it on silent – he hated to disturb other passengers, though few others seemed to care; there was no silent coach on this service – so he felt the vibrations in his pocket. He withdrew it. Fran.

'Good time, bad time?' she said.

'I'm on the train.'

'Oh.'

Robert checked his watch: almost quarter to eight. Early for Fran, in the holidays, especially now that the boys were teenagers. Adam was the early riser, wasn't he? Sometimes went out on his bike before the rest of the family were up; he'd told Robert this, shown him the Lycra outfit he wore, with a pride (it was true, he was fit, far fitter than Robert, though Robert wouldn't have cared if Adam had won ten Ironman competitions, so deep-seated was his dislike of the man) that had raised in Robert a faint distaste. He wondered if they'd had one of their arguments; he thought he could hear it in Fran's voice, that faint tremor, that brave, bright, soldiering tone.

'I thought you were off now,' his sister said. 'For Christmas.'

The train was easing to a halt; Robert's reply was swallowed by the slight commotion, the doors opening, closing again, a few people getting off, a woman getting on, wearing white trainers with her grey suit. The carriage was almost empty; most people, in accordance with Fran's assumptions, must have taken the whole week off.

'Tomorrow,' he said when the train pulled away. 'I'm off from tomorrow. Got a few things to tie up at the office.'

'Oh. Well. It was just to tell you that The Oaks called. Dad had a bad night. I'm going in now.'

That swallow swoop and flutter in his chest. He took a breath. She would surely have cut to the chase if the news was significant. 'How bad?'

'Oh, nothing too serious, I think. He's just a bit upset. Sharon thought it would help to see a familiar face. Though how familiar any of us are these days, I'm not so sure.'

'Sharon?'

He caught her faint sigh. 'Sharon – you know, the new one. Nice. Red hair. Tattoos.'

'Oh. Yes. Sharon.'

They entered a tunnel now; the carriage briefly darkened, and Robert didn't hear his sister's reply. He'd forgotten that the signal was iffy here – he so rarely used his phone on the train. When they emerged, into high, sharp winter light, the connection had been cut. He wrote Fran a message – *Thanks for the call, keep me posted. I'll ring later*. He hit send.

Robert watched the rows of terraces, all those Victorian brick boxes, with other, newer glass cubes attached to their rear ends. Admired the next bridge along as they crossed the river; the rivets and pillars and struts of steel, spanning the murky Thames. On the north bank the various ribboning tracks came together like water flowing to its source. There was beauty here, beauty in the minds of the engineers who'd designed the network and the workers who'd built it; beauty in the way the system ran, far more often smoothly than not, cogs turning within cogs, wheels within wheels. Robert lost himself for a moment in the professional pride this inspired in him, as he almost always did, no matter how many times he travelled this journey, back and forth.

It was only when the train had lurched to a stop at Victoria that he remembered his sister, and his message to her – unsent, he saw now, in that patch of poor signal – and then, with a sudden low grasp of panic, that he'd forgotten to buy her a Christmas present. How could he have done this? It was appalling; but he'd done it, there was no denying it, he'd forgotten Fran.

There were, as Robert saw it, two ways you could go after a childhood like theirs, a marriage like their parents'. You could, as he had, refuse to participate: not marry, not have children, not allow yourself to end up handcuffed to a life you barely recognised. No exit, no way out, just the weight of responsibility, of decisions taken and regretted.

He loved Della, of course, but he preferred to believe, each day that they were together, that their being together was an active choice, not a state decreed by law. There had been an anxious, painful time when it had become clear to him, to them both, that Della did not feel the same, that she wanted the things he did not. He still felt it, occasionally – the guilt, the knowledge that he had, in his intransigence, denied her something so elemental, so much a part of most people's lives. Marriage. Children. He worried sometimes that on some subconscious level Della resented him for this, though she insisted that this was not so. And yet Robert knew that he could not have chosen differently, could not have done so and remained true to who he was, to the life he wanted to live.

The other way, then, was the one Fran had chosen: to marry someone as manifestly unsuitable as their father had been for their mother, and re-enact the whole sad charade. Robert admired her for it, really; her reserves of optimism, of sheer energy, must run far deeper than his. For it was obvious, to Robert at least, that Fran was unhappy; how could she not be with a man like Adam Lytton, a man who talked down to her, insisted on taking charge, found fault with everything she did. And Robert and Della, of course, must see only the surface ripples; the under-tow, he was sure, must be stronger, deeper, far more treacherous.

Della thought he was far too invested in the state of his sister's marriage. They'd been together, Fran and Adam, for decades now – God, it must be coming up for twenty-five years – and Jesse was almost an adult, Dylan not far behind. But what Della didn't seem to understand was that Robert felt, in part, responsible for the fact that Adam and Fran had met at all. A party in Margate in the mid-1990s at Della's workspace, which formed part of a warehouse complex of artists' studios; they threw regular parties, there were no neighbours, and even if there had been, nobody, in that place and at that time, would have thought to complain. He'd invited Fran for the weekend – she was thirty-one, bored in her job, miserable in the wake of another break-up. (None of her relationships, as far as Robert knew, had lasted longer than six months.) God knew who'd invited Adam Lytton – he wasn't a part of the usual crowd. A property developer from Sheppey, which he called 'the island' – chippy, with a hatred of privilege, of everything he felt he hadn't had. All this Robert would learn later; that night, all he'd seen was a man with a narrow, raffish face, wearing a polo shirt and chinos, chatting up his sister. He couldn't have been more surprised when the next morning, over a late hungover breakfast in the flat in Cliftonville, Fran had announced that she was going out for the day with this man Adam for a drive along the coast. He'd arrived shortly afterwards in a convertible BMW, honked his horn down in the street; in she'd got, and that had been that.

At the wedding, Katherine had drunk too much champagne – the real stuff, Dom Perignon; Adam was already making money – and there had been a bit of a scene. She'd accosted Fran, flushed and corseted in her tight white long-trained wedding dress, and told her that she'd made a terrible mistake. Robert had seen it all – Fran's snarled reply, her tears, her flight from the marquee, off into the deep, unlighted shadows of the hotel grounds. A flurry of bridesmaids had pursued her; Robert had tackled their mother (who knew where Dad had got to?). Found her a glass of water, settled her in a gold spindled chair. She must have been in her seventies then – old for the mother of the bride, two decades older than Adam's mother, showily glamorous in her matching peach ensemble. The sight of Katherine Samuels in that moment: slumped on her chair, the glass of water in her hand, her hairdo loosening, her make-up smudged and bleeding, failing to hide her age and her unhappiness. 'I just don't want her to suffer like I have,' she said, and Robert held her hand, and spared her his unspoken thoughts. *You chose to marry Dad. You chose to have us. You could have chosen not to have children. You could have chosen to leave him. You chose it all.*

Fran never really forgave their mother; oh, they had spoken again, observed the outward niceties – Christmases, birthdays, time together after the boys were born – but it had never been the same between them. She'd admitted this to Robert at their mother's funeral; they'd sat up for hours in the bungalow after everyone had left, their father and the boys dispatched to bed, Della melting away, even Adam, brash and brittle as he was, understanding that his role, in this moment, was to disappear. Drinking whisky, a good bottle Robert had brought with him from home.

'I think I hated her, a little,' Fran said, some time in that long night. 'Or maybe quite a lot. Hated her and loved her, at the same time. Does that make any sense at all?'

Robert nodded. He looked at his sister, ten years his junior – he knew, now, that there had been losses in between, late-term miscarriages, authentic suffering; they both knew this, though neither could think who had told them, or when. A decade between them; he remembered the day Fran was born, the tiny, wrinkled bundle of her, and their mother's face pale and blue-veined against the hospital pillow. It had been a difficult birth – he'd known that, even at ten years old; knew by then, too, that everything was difficult for their mother, that for her life was a struggle, just getting through from day to day. Blamed her for it and pitied her, both at the same time; which was too much knowledge, surely, for a ten-year-old boy to hold.

'It does, Fran,' he said that night in the dark parental home, their father and their families asleep along the corridor, their mother gone, committed to ash, to air. 'It does to me.'

He left the office just after three; wished a happy Christmas to the last few stragglers on his floor and to Stan, the doorman, to whose home address he'd already had his secretary, Janice, dispatch two bottles of wine from Berry Bros. & Rudd.

The day was fading over the Strand. The lights were on, blinking stars and moons strung high above the road, above the buses and the taxis and the bicycles, above the heads of the pedestrians, buttoned into their coats and scarves, though it was not so cold today; a fine day really, a fine, darkening December afternoon with just a few days to go till Christmas. He still felt it, though he was a sixty-six-year-old man, past middle age, a company director with a mortgage, life insurance, assets and investments, and no children – bar dear Lizzy, who was grown herself now, anyway – to keep the traditions alive: the stockings, the pantomimes, the visits to Father Christmas in a department-store grotto. Still, he felt it: the lightness, the expansiveness, the anticipation, the sense that something good was coming. And it was, wasn't it – though Christine was gone, and missed; and Dad was in The Oaks; and the world was still licking its collective wounds; and there was still suffering every-where, suffering and loneliness and sadness. Despite all this, it was good: it was kindness, it was giving without thought of recompense, it was light in the darkness.

He'd called Fran at lunchtime, eating a Pret turkey and cran-berry sandwich at his desk. Dad was fine, she said, calm again, equanimity restored. She'd played Abe some music on the Bluetooth speakers they'd bought him the previous Christmas, when they had not been able to see him, when all Robert and Fran and Della (Adam hadn't bothered) had been able to do was record messages on their phones and have the staff play him their voices, disembodied, reading to him, offering him their small snippets of news. Abe had grown agitated listening, the nurses said – had just wanted to know where they all were, why nobody was coming to see him, so they'd stopped bothering with the recordings after a while. He liked the music, though – the nurses agreed that it helped penetrate the fog. He sang along today, Fran said, to Sinatra doing 'I'll Be Home for Christmas'. Turned to her afterwards, asked her what she was cooking for dinner this year: turkey or beef?

'I told him turkey,' Fran said over the phone. 'I suppose he thought I was Mum.'

'Yes,' Robert said, looking down at his half-finished sandwich. 'I suppose he did.'

Now he threaded his way along the Strand towards Trafalgar

Square; he had in mind the big Waterstones there, on the corner, the one on several floors. Hadn't Fran said to him just a few weeks ago that she hadn't been reading so much recently, that she missed the part-time job she'd had in her friend Maddy's bookshop on Market Square, that her favourite thing of all had been seeing the new novels coming in, boxes of them in their pristine jackets, and choosing the ones she wanted to take home for herself. He'd buy a stack of novels for her; he preferred non-fiction, wasn't terribly clued up on contemporary novelists, but he'd call Della, ask her advice, or perhaps the booksellers would help. They were good like that, knowledgeable; he came in quite often, browsing, seeking downtime from work. He could buy the whole Booker shortlist, maybe; it would be heavy, carrying the books home on the train, but he'd manage. He'd keep the receipt; any Fran had already read she could exchange.

Robert was approaching the square now; the dusk was deepening, the high Norwegian tree lit with shimmering blue strings of light. Robert took out his phone. 'I forgot Fran,' he told Della. 'A present, I mean. Can you believe it? I'm going to Waterstones now, before the train. There must be some novels she'd like. Can you help me choose?'

He heard her smile, lightening her voice, bringing that small rising inflection. How he loved the sound of Della's voice, how it lifted him, even after all this time, more than the lights, more than the tree, more than the small boy passing him now, holding his mother's hand; asking her, loudly and anxiously, how Father Christmas was going to get into their flat, given that they didn't have a chimney or a fireplace.

They had been good times, their family Christmases, when they were children; some of the best times, really, periods of stillness, of hostilities briefly set aside. Katherine busy in the kitchen, baking mince pies, stollen cake, gingerbread biscuits in the shape of stars; Robert and Fran had helped when they were little, put on oversized aprons and balanced on stools, placing the star-shaped cutter to the dough, their hands dusted with icing sugar. But no, this memory was false, there had never been a time when they had both been small enough to climb on adjacent stools: by the time Fran was a toddler, Robert was almost in his teens. Funny how memory did that – played tricks, laid invented images over true ones. Everyone remembered things differently anyway, though Fran, too – they had talked about it – remembered Christmas as the best of times.

It had been a kind of performance, Robert thought now, on all their parts. There'd been a Hanukah dinner for the Samuels grandparents: latkes and brisket, their grandfather lighting the menorah, all of them in their best clothes, the bungalow dining room transformed to a place of magic, of light and shadow, of mysterious ancient traditions neither Robert, nor Fran, nor their mother – nor, really, their father – fully understood. Then, once Grandma and Grandpa Samuels had been dispatched back to London, a Christmas party: neighbours and Rotary Club couples and Abe's fellow salesmen, spivvy types in braces and shiny shoes, their wives spritzed with perfume, wearing dresses of too-tight brocade.

Robert and Fran had been drafted in to help with the decorations – folding paper chains, hanging foil garlands from the light fittings – and then, once Fran had been reluctantly dispatched to bed, Robert had served the drinks and vol au vents, inviting friends from school as back-up. The adults had all got mildly – sometimes more seriously – drunk; drunk enough as the night wore on, anyway, not to notice Robert and his school-mates pouring themselves bucketfuls of Abe's punch. He'd got drunk himself for the first time at one of these parties – had thrown up discreetly in the upstairs bathroom, drawing his sister from her bed to stare at him from the doorway (she couldn't have been more than five or six), asking whether he was all right. 'I'm fine, Franny,' he'd croaked, 'go back to bed. Don't tell Mum and Dad, OK?' And she hadn't, she'd done exactly as he'd asked; had understood, even then, that their ultimate loyalty, in the face of their parents' inconsistencies, their mother's mood swings, the shouting and the tears and the all-too-brief recon-ciliations, must be to each other.

It was strange – Robert could hardly remember any of the people at these parties coming to the bungalow at any other time of year. His parents hadn't had many friends – it might have been better, he thought, if they had, might have offered each of them more of a foil against the shortcomings of the other. He didn't know where the crowds had appeared from each Christmas, fill-ing the kitchen and lounge, spilling out into the back garden, smoking their cigarettes, drinking their punch, shrieking with laughter; they might have been acquired from central casting, a herd of extras ushered in to set the scene. The Happy Sub-urban Couple, Throwing A Christmas Party For Their Friends. Katherine seeming, yes, happy: bright lipstick, a new dress, high heels, her hair curled and set; Abe sharing a cigar with the men from work, his shirt collar loosened, his face flushed.

The festive mood had continued into Christmas Day, which they'd spent with their maternal grandparents, the Symondses, either at the bungalow or at the Symonds' house in Penarth, with its view of the sea (years later, after meeting Della, after moving to Margate to be with her, Robert would look out over that other, opposite stretch of water and think of his grandparents' house on Cardiff Bay). His friends, on their return to school in the new year, reported arguments, sulks, even flaming rows over the turkey's denuded carcass; not so with them, everyone was on their best behaviour. Sometimes, when he was younger – before Fran had come along, anyway – Robert had allowed himself to believe that this was how it would be from now on, that something between his parents had finally shifted for the better. And perhaps it had; perhaps, for that fortnight or so in December, they, Abe and Katherine Samuels, had believed it too.

He was thinking of all this as he dressed for Fran and Adam's party; he'd been out in the garden all afternoon, chopping logs for the wood-burner (Della worried he'd do his back in, and he did get a bit sore afterwards, but he liked the physical labour, the necessary shift from all that sitting at a desk). Della had spent the afternoon in her studio – he knew she was working on something for him, but he was doing his best to play along. She had already showered and dressed; she was downstairs, pouring them both a gin and tonic – he'd just have the one, drive them into Lenbourne, abandon the car at Fran's, get a taxi home. Lizzy was coming, too; she'd be there any minute. They'd share the taxi, drop her home so she could get up in the morning with the dogs.

Yes, Robert thought, buttoning his shirt before the mirror, taking up his comb to tackle the bedraggled nest of his hair. He understood why Fran did this every year, as their mother had before her – threw a party, put herself through all the stress and the expense and the clearing-up. It was a way, wasn't it, to set aside whatever else was going on, whatever dissatisfactions and complexities defined the rest of one's life, one's lot. One evening, among all the others, to shine, and smile, and say to the world, or at least to family and friends: I'm here, I'm alive, and tonight, at least, I'm all right.

For Maddy

'You're sure there's nothing else I can bring?'

'Really there isn't. Adam ordered everything online. I'm surrounded by sausage rolls as I speak.' Economy sausage rolls, beside her on the worktop: two jumbo-sized packs, each tube of meat greyish and shrunken inside its desiccated pastry case. Between them was a vat of coleslaw and a carton of frozen Indian snacks.

Fran had been halfway through unpacking the shopping when Maddy called. The boys had melted away, and Adam was working until lunchtime, so there had been no one to whom Fran could express her renewed frustration with the fact that she had wanted to have the party catered, or at least order platters from Marks & Spencer, and instead Adam had gone ahead and bought everything online from Asda. 'There you go,' he'd said, presenting her with the order. 'All done. Nothing to stress about now, is there?' Grinning, looking so thoroughly delighted with himself that Fran could have hit him, right there in front of the boys.

But Fran hadn't hit Adam, of course, and she wasn't going to complain about any of this to Maddy now. It was unfashionable these days, loyalty – to husbands, to wives; to the concept of marriage, which still seemed to Fran a sacred one, in some mysterious undefinable way – but it still mattered to her.

'Well, that's good,' Maddy said. 'I'll bring a couple of bottles. Be there as soon as I can after closing. Sorry I can't come any earlier.'

Fran reached into the nearest plastic bag, drew out an enormous trifle. The custard had slipped into the cream and the jelly was smeared, blood-like, across the lid. How old did Adam think they all were – six? 'Don't be silly. We'll be in full swing when you get here, with any luck. Are you coming with Peter, then? The mysterious Peter Newton. Dark horses, both of you.'

Noises emerged at Maddy's end of the line. The high chime of the bell above the door (this sound had punctuated Fran's days in the bookshop, treasured days of stillness and dusty light and the glorious glue-and-resin scent of fresh books). The lilt of a child's voice, rising over the low burble of Maddy's music. *Mummy, mummy.* The music was Annie Lennox, that Christmas album she'd done a few years back; Fran had a copy, too, had put several tracks from it on her playlist for the party.

'Not so dark,' Maddy said. 'I didn't want to jinx it. I don't know what it is yet. But it's something. Maybe.'

'Definitely. Adam rates him. Says he's one of the good ones.'

'Ha. Well. That's good to know.'

The child in the bookshop was shouting now. *Mummy, I'm hungry. I'm hungry, Mummy!* A boy, it sounded like, maybe four or five. Jesse and Dylan at that age, quick and sleek as little mop-haired seals.

'Better go, Fran,' Maddy said. 'Customers. I'll see you tonight, OK?'

'OK. See you later.'

Fran stood still for a moment after hanging up. The bags were everywhere, filling the worktops and the island, spilling their contents on to the floor. They'd be eating leftover sausage rolls and mini quiches (she'd spotted three boxes of these so far) for months. Adam had meant well, of course, doing the shop for her – he always meant well. This was what she knew about Adam and others didn't. Some others, anyway. Robert, above all.

It was almost half past twelve; the boys would want lunch shortly, and Adam would be done not long after. There was the shopping to put away, and the house to tidy, and her dress to pick up from the dry cleaner's. Alice had promised to arrive early, with the girl she was bringing, to sort the drinks and the glasses, get the boys to help, give Fran time to have a shower before the party. The house looked all right; the decorations were up, they'd done them early this year, back at the beginning of December. Ordered a nine-footer, put it in its usual place in the bay window. Adam had gone up to the attic for the boxes of decorations and they'd arranged them together, the four of them, carols on Alexa and mince pies in the oven, like something from a John Lewis advert.

'Argos, more like, if Dad has anything to do with it,' Dylan had joked, and they'd all laughed, Adam too. He could laugh at himself, her husband; it was another thing Fran loved about him, always had, and that not everybody got to see.

Maddy liked Adam, and he liked her. Fran had discovered this early in their friendship, and it wasn't something she took for granted. She knew Adam was awkward in company, that he wore this almost as a badge of honour. 'I just don't like *pretending*,' he'd told her early on, and she'd respected him for it, reminded herself that a man who hated lies was better than the opposite.

Her previous boyfriend had lied to her – insisted he wasn't sleeping with his old girlfriend when he was – and the one before that, too. So much of everyone's lives, it had seemed to Fran then – thirty-one and single, the only one among her friends not to be married, not to be anywhere near having kids – was built on lies. Her parents' lives above all: the lie of a happy marriage, the lie of a happy mother. Katherine had never wanted Fran and Robert, believed that they'd ruined her figure, her career; that they'd stolen her looks and her time and her peace of mind. She'd never said any of this aloud, but Fran had understood it all. Adam refuted such mendacity; he was always utterly and entirely himself. A bit impossible some of the time, perhaps; but at least even then he wasn't trying to be someone, or something, he wasn't.

Fran had got talking to Maddy in the bookshop not long after it had opened. The ladies' boutique on Market Square had been derelict for years. A pair of dusty naked mannequins still stood in the window; Fran had passed them morning and afternoon with the boys, walking to and from school. She had watched the bookshop emerge over a period of months: the mannequins removed, the old sign – *James's Fine Clothing* – replaced, the weatherboarding sanded and repainted.

The other mums agreed that the arrival of a bookshop was an excellent thing, a sign of Lenbourne's incipient regeneration. Next, someone said, there'd be a hipster coffee shop, and after that it was only a matter of time until they got a Waitrose. Fran was dubious but agreed that a new bookshop was worth celebrating. She loved reading, devoured novel after novel in the hours between shopping and tidying and hanging out the washing and taking it in and cooking and loading the dishwasher and unloading it again. There was actually a good number of such hours at her disposal. They had a cleaner, Adam insisted on that: Fran was staying home to be there for the boys, not a skivvy. But these empty hours had begun to weigh on Fran with a heaviness that unsettled her; that made her think, frighteningly, of her mother.

It had been easy, then, to step into the new bookshop one afternoon and find Maddy standing there, a woman of about her own age, her dark hair cut into a smooth bob, her brown eyes warm beneath her fringe. Their connection had been immediate, at least for Fran; she'd returned again and again, bought half the shop, stood there chatting for so long she'd been late several times picking up the boys. Fran had suggested a coffee, then Maddy had invited her for drinks at the wine bar across the square; it had seemed natural to Fran, after that, to mention dinner at home, though she'd done so not without misgivings. It was so easy for Adam to rub people up the wrong way. She'd lost several friends over the years following uneasy dinners, and a couple of weekends away during which some kind of argument had broken out, and the friend had taken offence, and Fran had had no choice but to take Adam's side. They didn't tend to holiday with friends now; it was easier, really, just to go away on their own. Adam was always more relaxed when it was just the four of them; the annual Christmas party was a rare exception, and one she knew he only tolerated because it mattered to her.

Maddy, then, had come for a barbecue one summer evening. Cool in a long green dress, brown-leather sandals; Fran had felt overdressed, too much like a provincial mum in her white capri pants and glittery ecru jumper (beige, if she was honest: it was beige). Maddy had handed Adam the bottle of Aperol she'd brought and said gently, 'I'd murder one of these, please, with a splash of prosecco, if you've got any. Would that be all right?'

Fran watched Adam look from the bottle to Maddy, wondering, uneasily, what he was going to say. But he'd only smiled, and said, 'Coming right up. I'll do one for all of us, shall I?'

Maddy grinned. 'Thank you.' To Fran, she added, 'Good man.'

'Yes,' Fran said. 'I think so.'

Maddy had stayed late that night: until midnight, the garden lights glowing, uplighting the high, still trees. A coolness in the air; they'd put blankets round their shoulders, lowered their voices so as not to disturb the neighbours or the boys asleep upstairs. Both women were a little drunk when Maddy left – not Adam, he never drank more than a couple. Maddy was going to walk home – it wasn't far – but Adam insisted on driving her. Fran sat on alone in the garden while he was gone, finishing her glass of wine, enjoying the night's rare stillness. When he returned, Adam said, 'Nice woman, that Maddy. Nice way about her. That ex-husband of hers must be mad.'

Fran nodded. 'I'm glad you liked her. I think she could become a good friend.'

He watched her for a moment. 'Were you so worried I wouldn't?'

'Maybe a little.' She got up, went over and kissed him; and they stood there for a moment, their foreheads pressed together, not speaking, not moving, just breathing the same air.

Adam had bought Fran a gift for Maddy, for them both, early in December, the same weekend they'd decorated the tree. He loved to do this, arrange a surprise that was not of her choosing and then present her with it. A form of control – Fran knew it for what it was – but also a form of love.

The gift was a holiday: a weekend in Lisbon, just the two of them, Maddy and Fran, to be taken between January and March the following year. A four-star hotel, with a view of the Atlantic;

there were grainy photographs on the prepaid voucher, issued by one of the discount companies to whose daily briefings Adam subscribed. There had been many such vouchers over the years – spa treatments; London theatre trips; a hot-air-balloon ride over Ashford. Fran's gratitude, in each case, had been tempered by a slight feeling of unease: the voucher always had strings, limitations; there was always, without fail, an awkward conversation with the manager. Fran did not, in all honesty, much like surprises, but Adam liked giving them, and so they continued. Churlish, anyway, to mind; she was lucky, they all were, Fran, Adam and the boys, with their lovely comfortable house, their lovely comfortable lives; and who could really complain about her husband booking a girls' weekend away?

And yet Fran worried a little: worried that Maddy would struggle to arrange time off; worried about being so far away from Dad, though of course Robert would be on hand, and if anything happened Fran could always fly home; worried that Maddy wouldn't like the hotel, which Fran had looked up online – the ratings weren't great, the rooms small. Ungrateful, again, but if she were to have pictured herself and Maddy in Lisbon at all she'd have placed them in some arty B&B, painted shutters and a terrace on which they could sit into the small hours, drinking bone-cold *vinho verde*. But they'd do that anyway; they'd drink wine, they'd climb the steep cobbled streets, they'd have a wonderful time. There was a bookshop in Lisbon, Fran knew, a famous one, with intricate wood panelling and a high, curving stair. She'd found a card online with a photograph – she would present this to Maddy as her gift, with the voucher tucked inside.

They were very different women, really; it surprised Fran, sometimes, that she and Maddy should have grown so close. Fran could, and did, talk to anyone about anything; Maddy was so contained, she gave so little away. When, for instance, Maddy had called to let Fran go in those awful early months of the pandemic, she'd been short with her, almost unkind. 'You never really needed the job, did you?' she'd said. 'I mean, it's not as if you're short of money.'

Fran, hanging out washing in the garden, the phone clamped between her shoulder and her ear – it was such a fine spring that year, so incongruously fine – had drawn a tight, uncomfortable breath. Embarrassment, of course – Maddy's, and her own, for the fact that business arrangements had crept into their friendship (she was being sacked, for goodness' sake!) – and Maddy's anxiety about the future. Everyone was anxious then. So Fran had forced brightness; she was good at that. 'No, no,' she said. 'You're right. We don't need the money. We'll be fine. I understand, Maddy. Don't worry about it. Not for a second.'

A kind of despair had settled over Fran for a while after this, though she'd chided herself, again: the whole country was despairing, people were sick and dying, everything was closed, they were all out on their doorsteps clapping and banging pans to honour those who risked their lives every day just going to work. Fran didn't risk her life each day, did she? She was lucky, she was fine. She worried about Abe – hated not being able to see him, hug him, hold his hand – but the boys were OK, did their work most of the time when she could tear them away from their computer games, and Adam's money was still coming in – construction had halted on the new housing developments, but he still had his private tenants, there was still rent to collect. Outwardly, Fran remained bright, shiny, can-do; she baked bread, posted photographs of her efforts, organised family quizzes, continued helping Maddy build a virtual presence for the shop. But inwardly Fran slumped; she missed the job, the hours out of the house, the boxes of books, the chats with Maddy. Missed Maddy herself, coming down from the flat upstairs in her dresses and sandals, smiling as she pushed open the door.

Fran envied her, really; envied Maddy's aloneness, her quiet rooms above the shop, everything ordered and still. No husband, no kids. Nobody to report to, nobody else's chaos to resolve. There was loneliness there – Maddy had admitted this in one or other of their conversations – but even that, sometimes, Fran envied; for what was that, really, but an admission of the fact that there was nobody to whom you were ultimately answerable? And sometimes, surely, there was relief in that.

The first of the guests would be here soon. Millie and Dave from next door; they usually shot round as soon as Fraser was down, keen to make the most of their babysitter's ticking clock. Then Patrick, Adam's partner, and his wife Corey – *second* wife, Fran should say; it was a few years now since he'd divorced Elaine. Corey was tall, reed-slender, with a mane of red-brown hair – she reminded Fran of a racehorse, had that thoroughbred elegance and nervy, bridled energy.

Dylan had put on the playlist downstairs. Strains of it travelled up to Fran, applying eyeliner at her dressing table. John Lennon's voice, strummed guitars, the faint clash of bells. Fran had hugged her younger son earlier, as he set up her laptop, and he'd melted into her for just a second, then pulled away; he was awkward at fifteen, his limbs gangling, his chin shadowed by uneven incipient fluff. A couple of his mates were coming later – Lewis and Dan – and Jesse's Alice was already there, with the girl she worked with at the café, drafted in to help; Fran was paying all of them, had put her foot down about that, and about bringing in an extra pair of hands. Chloe was the girl's name: Peter Newton's daughter, as it happened. She seemed like a nice girl – a little wild, perhaps, her red hair loose across her shoulders, wearing fishnet tights and DMs beneath her short black skirt. But nothing Maddy wouldn't be able to handle, Fran was sure.

Alice really was the dictionary definition of a nice girl. Pretty and sensible, and clever, too; she had her sights set on Medicine at Oxford, was heading for three As. Brighter than Jesse, though of course Fran would never dream of voicing this; his ambitions were more modest, he was hoping for business studies, Oxford Brookes. He and Alice wanted to rent a little house together in Jericho, they already had it all planned out. They were in the same class at the grammar, had been together two years so far.

Adam adored Alice – no small thing – and Fran did too, really, though there was a small, whispering part of her that would have loved to see Jesse make a more unexpected choice. A girl more like Chloe – someone with tattoos and a part-shaved head, or whatever stood as the markers of rebellion these days; or a boy even, a fellow striker on the Lenbourne Under-18s. But no: Jesse planned to marry Alice, to return to Lenbourne eventually, where Alice would work as a GP and Jesse would work for his dad. Adam even had his eye on a house for them – a section of the creekside shipwrights he was in the process of acquiring, close to Jackson's. Alice had shown Fran the pictures she was collecting on her phone as inspiration: kitchens and bathrooms and utility rooms, everything artfully arranged, everything in its place. It was laudable, of course, to have such plans, such clear ideas; but Alice was seventeen, for goodness' sake, they both were. Fran, at their age, had still been thinking about nothing much more than perms and cherry lip-gloss and whether she would ever marry Simon Le Bon. Perhaps, she reminded herself now, that was why she was just a postmenopausal housewife with a grumpy husband, a flabby tummy and two teenage sons who, in a few short years, would have moved out, leaving herself and Adam here alone.

Fran pouted at her reflection – matt Chanel rather than cherry gloss, though she worried that matt was too ageing, too stark against the fine lines that cross-hatched her face; despite her monthly anti-ageing facials, she could still see them, didn't think the expensive treatments had had the slightest effect. John Lennon had been replaced by Wings doing 'Mull of Kintyre'; she'd thought it a good segue, though she could hear Dylan complaining from the floor below. The house, grandly Victorian, was appallingly badly soundproofed – you could hardly cough without being overheard, and if you opened the front windows in summer you were deafened by the noise from the Canterbury Road. It had been Adam's choice, really; sometimes, when she stopped to think about it – which Fran didn't, not really; not too often, anyway – it seemed that almost everything about their lives had been Adam's choice.

Fran put down her lipstick, sat for a moment, her hands in her lap. Her mother's face stared back at her: pale, wispy-blonde, the corners of her lips downturned. Blood-red lipstick, bare décolletage, a glitzy party dress. Though she had already been put to bed, Fran had sometimes watched her mother getting ready for the annual Christmas party at the bungalow, spying through a crack in the door. Katherine had usually caught her, and then dragged her, really quite roughly, back to bed; it was Dad who'd been the gentle one. Fran had sat with him in his room at The Oaks earlier in the week, talking to him, offering him scraps of news, stroking his hand. Strange, to miss a person who was still there, still living, but there it was. She'd be back to see him tomorrow – Christmas Eve – and she'd pop by on

Christmas Day, too – both of them would, Fran and Robert, sister and brother, daughter and son. Wishing Abe a happy Christmas, a happy Hanukah; helping him tear the wrapping off gifts he would hardly notice, let alone use. Concealing their sadness with busyness, with bright smiles and paper hats; for what else, in the end, could either of them do?

The party was going well – better than usual, better than ever, maybe. It had been two years since the last one, and the mood was doubly buoyant; the talk seemed louder, the laughter brighter, the alcohol more plentiful. Fran drifted from kitchen to living room to garden (they had the patio heaters on), un-tethered, freeform. She talked to Millie from next door about potty-training (she was having trouble with Fraser); to Corey about a tricky operation she'd just helped perform on a French bulldog with breathing problems; to Alan and Louise, Alice's mum and dad, about the cruise to the Faroes they'd booked for the following spring.

Robert and Della arrived with Lizzy. Fran caught her by the shoulders, already a little tipsy on the prosecco Alice, Chloe and the boys were liberally resupplying. 'How are you *doing*, lovely?' she whispered into Lizzy's ear – she really was lovely, young and gorgeous in a black jumpsuit, trainers and a fake fur shrug.

Lizzy returned Fran's embrace. 'I'm all right, thank you. More or less. But yes, I'm doing OK.'

Lizzy's words spun through Fran's mind like a mantra as the party ran on. Towards nine, Maddy arrived with the famous Peter – tall and handsome in a crumpled, pepper-and-salt kind of way (he reminded Fran of that gardener on the telly – the posh one – Donny Mont. No – she must be more than a little tipsy now – Monty Don). Some time after that, Dylan switched Fran's Christmas playlist for his own, all rumbling bass and electronic beeps, and was then firmly instructed by his father to switch it back.

We're doing OK, Fran thought, floating once more, living room to kitchen and garden and back again. *We're all doing OK.*

At some point in the evening – quite late; the night was black and chilly, the heaters failing to disperse the frigid air – Fran found herself standing outside on the decking with Maddy, sharing a cigarette. Maddy's pack: Fran hardly ever smoked. Through an agreeable haze of drunkenness, Fran remembered Maddy's card, Maddy's gift; she threaded her way back through the house, retrieved it from the hallway table. Outside, she pressed the card into Maddy's hand.

'Thank you,' Maddy said. 'Should I open it now, or wait?'

'Up to you. Adam had a hand in it, to be honest. It was his idea. But I think you'll like it. I hope you will, anyway.'

'Intriguing.'

Maddy was casual in jeans, white shirt and grey jumper – she'd come straight from the bookshop. But Fran could see that she'd taken care with her make-up – she was wearing eye-liner, shadow, lipstick – and there was a certain radiance about her, a glow. Peter, Fran supposed; that possibility, the sense that something interesting, even transformative, was about to begin. And Fran hoped it was, she really did. She didn't envy it, not really – well, only a little.

'I'll wait, I think,' Maddy said, slipping her lighter back into her pocket. 'Keep the surprise for Christmas Day. I put your present under the tree. Which is looking lovely, by the way. The whole house is.'

Fran smiled, passed back the cigarette. 'Thanks. Adam helps. And the boys.'

Maddy nodded. 'Three good men.'

A fine trail of smoke clouded from Maddy's lips: Fran watched it hanging on the cool air, then rising, vanishing. She was cold out here without her coat; in a minute she would go in, they both would, refill their glasses, melt back into the throng, for it was crowded now, the house, everyone they'd invited had come and brought others, too. Even Adam seemed to be enjoying himself: the last time Fran had seen him he was in the living room, pouring Eddy from Valley Motors a measure of brandy, laughing about something, some joke Fran had been too late to catch. Eddy, beside him, had been smiling in response. A few feet away, Daniela, Eddy's wife – she'd used to clean for them, Ilona was really no match – was talking to Millie; Fran, as she'd passed, had caught the words 'potty' and 'poo'.

Maddy passed back the cigarette and Fran drew in a final drag, crushed the stub beneath her heel. 'Come on,' she said. 'Let's go back in. It's like the bloody Arctic out here.'

They stepped back into the kitchen. Maddy went on into the hallway, looking for Peter, Fran supposed; she hung back, taking in the flotsam: the dirty glasses, the half-eaten sausage rolls, the bowls of congealing trifle mush. Alice and Jesse were at the sink, washing up. Fran shooed them away. 'For God's sake, you two. Don't worry about that now. Go and have fun.'

They did as they were told, turned towards the garden. 'Thanks, Ma,' Jesse said – he was so tall, her elder boy, more than six foot, a good three inches taller than his father – and kissed her on the cheek as he passed.

'Happy Christmas, Mrs Lytton,' Alice said, and Fran wished her the same.

In a moment, someone would straggle through from the living room, where the chatter and the music were still going strong – Annie Lennox now, her version of 'In the Bleak Midwinter', not exactly a party classic, but lovely all the same – seeking food, wine, beer. For now, though, just for now, Fran was alone; she stood beside the island, reached again for the bottle, topped up her glass. She would ignore the chaos; there would be time enough tomorrow for the clear-up. They'd stay in their pyjamas all day, the four of them (or five, if Alice stayed), eat mince pies and chocolate, watch the carols from Cambridge on the telly: just another Christmas Eve, with all its tarnished gloss, its ordinary magic.

Fran thought of Maddy, opening her card on Christmas Day; then later, sitting across the table from Peter in the Plough, raising her glass to his. She thought of her brother and Della; of Lizzy; of Lizzy's mother, Christine. She thought of Abe, eating his turkey dinner in The Oaks dining room; of Sharon placing a paper hat on his balding, shiny head, his hair so fine and sparse, his skull as bare and vulnerable as a newborn's.

She thought of Adam, who loved her, and whom she loved, no matter the complexities, the compromises their mode of love entailed. She thought about how much they needed this, all of them, even those, like her, who drew from it no religious resonance; this homespun, patched-together festival and its counterparts – her grandparents' Hanukah; Diwali, and the winter solstice, and Chinese New Year, or just a piss-up in an all-night lock-in somewhere. What had the Romans called it – Saturnalia? The word floated to her across the decades, from some almost-forgotten afternoon in school. Miss Thomas's history class. Teenage boredom, the scent of armpits and hairspray, Miss Thomas scratching away in green chalk. *Saturnalia*. The Roman festival, marking the seasonal tilt away from darkness towards the light. Gifts given, gifts received. Love offered, love mourned. The comfort of ritual. A pause. A drawn breath. A moment of stillness in the world's ongoing spin.

ACKNOWLEDGEMENTS

It may come as no surprise to readers that I love Christmas. Really love it, for all its pressures and stresses, its commercialism and its tawdry glitter. So my first thanks must go to my mum, Jan Bild, for always making our Christmases feel special, no matter what was going on in our lives at the time.

With regards to the researching, writing, editing and publishing of this novel, I'd like to thank Judith Murray, Federico Andornino, Sally Oliver, Virginia Woolstencroft, Helen Crawford-White, Toksi Osunsade, Andy Glen, Laura Tache, Kit Gillet, Cristina Frangulea and John Doe.

Although the town of Lenbourne and its surrounding area is fictionalised, it is partly inspired by Faversham, Swale and the north Kent coast and marshlands. I moved to the area from south London in 2020 (quite a change) and find it both beautiful – even when the snow is so thick that the fields look like Arctic tundra – and creatively inspiring. I couldn't have set this novel anywhere else. I'd like to thank our new local friends for making us feel so welcome – particularly Christabel Greenaway and Tom Whitnell; Simon Tyler of Creekside Vinyl and Annabel Tullberg; and Rachel Thapa-Chhetri of Top Hat & Tales / Tales on Market Street.

To Andy and Caleb: we've had one Christmas together so far,

in the middle of a pandemic, in our chilly, crumbling new house in a field, and it still managed to be the best one ever. Here's, I hope, to many, many more.

LB

What if the family you want . . .

. . . isn't the family you need?

Read an extract from Laura Barnett's new novel
This Beating Heart

Once upon a time, there was a man and a woman.

The man and the woman fell in love. They walked in parks, held hands across restaurant tables. They moved in together. The woman forgave the man for his obsessive tidiness and secret collection of boxed *Star Trek* figurines, and the man overlooked the woman's grumpiness when tired and tendency to ignore the conspicuous build-up of dust balls.

The man and the woman got married. The woman stopped taking the pills she kept in the drawer of her bedside table, and the man left the last of the little plastic packets on his own side of the bed untouched.

The man and the woman spent a lot of time in bed, and the woman spent a lot of time looking at the calendar on her phone.

Time passed. Each month, the woman bled and cried a little, and the man held her close and told her that it would surely happen soon. It had happened, after all, for almost all their friends and colleagues and cousins and acquaintances, and all the buggy-pushing, sling-wearing people everywhere, on every pavement, every Tube train, in the park the man and the woman still liked to walk in at weekends.

Eventually, the man said, it will happen for us. The woman began not to believe him, but she let him tell her what she wanted to hear, and she let him hold her, because she wanted, above everything, to be held.

It did not happen, not in the way the man said it would. What happened, instead, were needles, and specialists, and blood pulsing on grainy pixelated screens. What happened was life stirring in Petri dishes, under microscopes. What happened was the woman injecting herself, and spreading her legs on hospital trolleys, and losing too many hours on the internet; and the man staring out of windows, waiting, letting his mind go blank until he could admit no thinking at all.

What happened was, not this time. What happened was, let's try again.

Time passed. Two lives quickened into being and were lost. The woman cried, and the man was mostly silent, and did his crying where nobody else could see.

The man and the woman began to shout at each other, and then stop, and then shout some more.

The man said, *No more*. The woman said, *One last time*.

The man and the woman stopped shouting at each other, and the silence this left behind was louder than any sound they had heard before.

The man left, taking half their things with him. His things. The woman stayed, in a half-furnished rented flat with a room she wouldn't enter, a door she kept closed.

This is the story of what happened next.

One

The playground was busy. Four o'clock on a London Tuesday afternoon: low autumn sunshine, rusting drifts of leaves. Crowds at the school gates; grey-haired women in high-vis jackets stopping traffic, waving their small, uniformed charges across the road.

Bev, she was called, the woman outside Wilberforce Primary: she'd been there for years, knew the children by name, most of the parents, too. Even Christina, and she was only there once a week, which hardly counted. But to Bev, apparently, it did. 'Hello there, Aunty,' Bev said with a smile as Christina crossed, gripping the children's hands so tightly that Gabriel complained that she was crushing his fingers, and wrenched free. It was only then, chasing Gabriel towards the park, Leila's hand still in hers, that Christina realised that Bev must have been speaking to her.

'Why,' Leila said, Gabriel still streaking out ahead, 'didn't you tell Bev that you're not really our aunty?'

'Gabriel! Stay where I can see you, please.' Then, to Leila, 'I didn't realise she was talking to me. And anyway, it doesn't matter if she thinks that, does it? I'm kind of your aunty, aren't I?'

'Not really.' Leila, dawdling, drew a line on the pavement

with the toe of her boot. 'Our Aunty Lizzie lives in Sheffield, with Uncle Rob, and Gracie and Oliver and Owen the baby. But we haven't met him yet.'

'I know she does. I know you haven't. But I . . .' Christina wasn't sure what defence to offer in addition, or why; it didn't matter, anyway, as now Gabriel was pushing open the gate to the playground, and Leila was letting go of her hand and running off after him.

She sat on her usual bench under the high, spreading horse chestnut tree, watching Gabriel scale the rope ladder and Leila follow another girl of a similar size – Lina, was it? Christina was sure she'd seen her here before – up the steps to the summit of the slide. When she'd first begun collecting Leila and Gabriel from school, she'd found the playground terrifying – dangers on all sides, everything far larger and higher than anything she could remember from her own childhood. Surely that rough surface wasn't safe; if a child fell off that rope bridge they'd break an arm, or worse. She'd hovered close to the children, not quite preventing herself from squealing out loud each time they attempted one of their simian ascents. This had lasted until one Saturday afternoon when she'd accompanied Jen and the children to the park, demoted to second-in-command; observing Christina's anxious hovering, Jen had insisted they find a bench to sit on, let the kids do their thing. 'We'll keep an eye, but don't worry, Chris – they're not made of glass.'

Oh, but they are, Christina had wanted to say. *They really are.* She watched them now. Leila was at the bottom of the slide, racing back to the steps for another turn. Gabriel had reached the prow of the pirate ship; Christina waved, and he waved back, then dived out of sight.

'How old?' a woman said. Christina looked round: a buggy, a green parka, a blue striped top. Mid-thirties, or thereabouts:

blonde hair, no make-up, but one of those faces that don't need it: wholesome, milk-fed. The baby appeared to be a girl; she stared at Christina, unblinking, from above a red duffel coat, navy tights, tiny shoes buckled with silver stars.

'Six,' Christina said. 'His sister's nine.'

The woman smiled. Her legs were narrow in her skinny jeans, her stomach flat. And the baby, what, six months? Eight? How had she done it? Luck, or breastfeeding, or starving herself? Luck, Christina decided: she had that look about her. Everything smooth, everything easy. Though you could never really tell, could you? No, assumptions could always deceive.

'Such lovely ages,' the woman said.

'Yes.' Christina mustered a reciprocal smile; she was just deciding whether to say more when the woman leant forward, tapped her on the belly. 'And how long,' she said, 'till this little one's ready to meet the world?'

Christina flinched, shook her head. The woman removed her hand. 'Oh God. I'm so sorry, I . . . I shouldn't have . . .'

'It's all right,' Christina said. 'It's fine. Really. Don't worry about it.' And then she stood and turned away, calling Jen's children, telling them it was time to head for home.

'Cow,' Jen said. 'I'd have slapped her round the face.'

'No you wouldn't. She felt bad enough as it was.'

'So she bloody well should have.'

Jen reached for the bottle of wine, refilled Christina's glass. They were in Jen's living room, the kids asleep down the hall, Christina's plate of reheated fish pie abandoned, uncleared, in the kitchen. 'Sod that,' Jen had said when she'd come in, throwing her padded coat over a chair, her hair in a high, loosening bun, her body, as she drew Christina into a tight embrace, smelling of deodorant and cigarettes and the low, musky whiff of drying sweat. 'I'm knackered, and I bet you are too, looking after those monkeys all afternoon. Come and sit with me. There's a posh bottle in the fridge. Chablis, I think. Mum went to Waitrose. Lucky us.'

Christina sipped her wine and said, 'I'm giving this dress to the charity shop. I don't think I can ever wear it again.'

'Oh Chris,' Jen said, laying her head on Christina's shoulder. 'The woman's an idiot. You don't look remotely pregnant.'

The word hung between them for a moment, its presence solid, almost tangible. Jen straightened, looked at her. Christina forced a smile. 'Tell me more about rehearsals. Is it coming together? Is Louis still being a pain?'

Jen waited a moment before replying, still watching her with that searching, clear-eyed gaze. Then she stretched and yawned, arching her back like a cat. 'He wasn't as bad today. Not quite, anyway. It was good. It's kind of . . . coalescing. I hope so, anyway. We've only got two weeks to go.'

'You'll pull it off. You always do.'

Later, they embraced in the hallway, under the ancient, blooming, ceiling water stain: the flat was a dump, Jen was always claiming she was looking for somewhere better, but nothing better ever seemed to appear. Nothing she could afford, anyway. 'Thank you, darling, as always, for today. I'm so grateful. You know that, don't you?'

Christina nodded, retrieved her handbag from the floor, drew it over her shoulder. 'I do know that. But really, it's a pleasure. We have fun.'

'I know you do. They love you.'

Leila earlier, on the way home from the park: taking Christina's hand again, and saying in a high, clear voice, *I wish you*

206

were our real aunty. I like you more than Aunty Lizzie. She smiled. 'I love them too.'

Christina followed Jen to the door, hung back as she opened it. The outside air smelt of damp leaves and, faintly, unemptied bins: it was bin day tomorrow, Christina had wheeled them out onto the pavement herself earlier, after she'd given the children their tea. Her own collection was the following day; she'd have to remember, it had been Ed's thing, it was so easy to forget.

'Have you spoken to Ed yet?' Jen said as Christina stepped out onto the path. Black and white chequers, original, weeds springing up around the missing tiles. 'About . . . Well. What happens next.'

Christina shook her head. 'Not yet.'

Jen leant against the door. She'd taken her hair down: it hung in glossy black coils around her shoulders. Backlit by the hall light, her loose, easy beauty was thrown into stark relief, her face divided by planes of shadow. A drawing by – what was his name? Schiele, Christina thought, or something like that: half mad, wasn't he; German or something, sketched dancers sitting tying their shoes. No, Austrian – they'd seen an exhibition in Vienna that weekend years ago, she and Ed. He'd grown restless, wandered off towards the café, while Christina had stayed, walking from painting to painting, taking the measure of each one: each woman's pale skin and reddish hair, her own particular blend of frailty and strength.

Jen blew her a kiss. 'I'll see you at Emma's on Saturday, right?'

'You will,' Christina said. 'Love you. See you then.'

Something woke Christina in the night. She lay stricken for a long moment, the rush of blood loud in her ears. The sound came again: a rustle, a crunch. Footsteps on gravel, just beyond the French windows. *Shit.* Her pulse redoubled; she could feel her heart thudding in her chest. She reached across the cool expanse of sheet to the empty pillow, felt beneath it for the hammer, gripped the handle in her hand. Its solidity was reassuring; she lay still, forcing herself to breathe. Nothing. A fox, a cat. Breathe.

Nobody knew about the hammer: she'd placed it there not long after Ed had moved out, under the pillow she'd also left on his side of the bed. There had been a spate of burglaries: Mrs Jackson upstairs had urged her to take care. 'Two women alone,' she'd said. 'We can't be too careful.' Christina, without thinking, had opened her mouth to rebut this – she, at any rate, was not alone – and then closed it again. The truth, of course, was that she was. That night, she'd found the hammer in the Ikea toolkit (Ed had left her this, taken the better one with him, the one he'd bought from B&Q), and put it under the adjacent pillow.

That noise again. Crunch, skitter, rustle. *Fuck.* There was definitely something there. Christina's breath stilled in her throat. Finding the light, swinging her legs round onto the carpet. Standing, carrying the hammer. Crunch of gravel. Thud of blood. She crossed the room, switched on the outside light, drew back the curtains, ready for ... what? A face, a body, danger in human form. But there was nothing, no one. Just the off-black London night, the patio slabs set in their bed of gravel, the herbs and rangy geraniums in tubs. Then that sound again, a stirring, and there it was: a hedgehog, scuttling off towards the concealing safety of darker shadows.

Christina lowered the hammer, light-headed with relief. For God's sake. She hadn't seen a hedgehog in years, and never here: her dad had encouraged them into the garden in Carshalton, left out water and cat food, built something he'd called a hedgehog hotel out of a plastic storage box covered with grass and straw. She didn't know whether any had ever moved in, but he'd liked to have it ready for them, just in case. That was just the sort of man her dad had been.

Christina closed the curtains, switched off the light. Sat on the edge of the bed, the hammer still in her hand. Then she placed it on the carpet, climbed back into bed, and lay with the lamp on for a few moments, watching the ceiling, letting her breath grow steady, her pulse slow.

'All well, darling?' her mother said.

Eleven o'clock on Thursday. Christina, at her desk, swivelled her chair away from her laptop screen, towards the wall: the framed graduation photo (Christina, Emma and Jen, in red lipstick and mortar boards, below the high neo-Gothic spires of Whitworth Hall); the bookcase lined with her files and reference books. This, the second bedroom, had survived Ed's departure more or less intact. Only Ed's collection of vintage sci-fi figurines – Darth Vader, Jabba the Hut, ET and others Christina couldn't name, each kept pristine in its box – had disappeared from the bottom of the built-in cupboard where Christina stored the piles of clothes she could no longer fit into, in the belief – optimistic or misguided, she could never quite decide – that one day, again, she would.

'Mum,' she said, 'it's the middle of the day. I'm working.'

'Sorry.' Then, a little pertly, 'You answered the phone, darling. You can't be that busy.'

There was no answer to this. Why hadn't she ignored the call? Boredom, she supposed – boredom, and silence, and habit:

the ingrained fear of missing something important, some vital news about Dad. Though, of course, now there was no more such news.

'OK, Mum. What is it? Everything all right with you?'

'Oh yes, darling. Yes. I was just calling to check whether you're still coming for lunch on Sunday.'

Christina shifted back to her laptop, the open Excel spreadsheet, the window beyond. Another fine, washed-clean autumn morning, the oak tree shedding its red and yellow leaves onto the lawn. She'd sweep the leaves up later; she still had all her gardening tools in the shed. They'd agreed that Ed wouldn't touch them: he would have no need of them in America, and anyway, most of them had been her dad's. For as long as she could remember, gardening had been their shared love; she'd had no choice in the matter, Dad had taken her outside with him the moment she'd been tall enough to hold a rake. Long hours together, digging, pruning, planting: all those small acts of tenderness, of care. So much easier, somehow, to do this for a garden than for yourself.

'Yes, I'm still coming, Mum. Why?'

A longish pause. Then, brightly, Sue said, 'Oh, no reason, darling. I was just . . .'

'Just what?'

'Well. You see, I've had this invitation . . .'

'Who from?'

'Oh, a few people from my dance class are going for lunch. There's a new Indian on the high street. They do an all-you-can-eat on Sundays. It really is unbelievable value. But of course, darling, I'd love to see you . . .'

'Mum, it's fine. Go to your lunch. Have fun. I'll come another time.'

'Well, darling, if you're sure. It would be nice to go with them.

The weekend after, then?' Sue paused: Christina pictured her standing in the kitchen, tethered to the phone (her parents had never got round to investing in cordless models), consulting the month-to-view wall calendar. Colin Prior's Scotland: Christina had bought it for her the previous Christmas, thinking of the holidays they'd taken together, the three of them, to Skye, Loch Lomond, Glencoe. But her mother, unwrapping it, had smiled politely and set it aside: too much, Christina had presumed, regretting her choice; too much to remember, too much to miss.

'Actually,' her mother said now, 'I have a cinema trip booked that Sunday. With the dance class. They're showing *The Red Shoes* at the British Film Institute. You know, the place in town, on the South Bank.'

'Yes, Mum, I know.'

Christina couldn't remember the last time her mother had gone 'into town': as far as Christina was aware, the boundaries of her life stretched no further than Croydon, Sutton, Cheam and, on rare occasions, Wimbledon, for the shopping centre, the Common, the smarter coffee shops. Sue had started this dance class in the spring – her friend Helen, a fellow widow, had started going, insisted it had changed her life. And her mother did seem to be changing: these plans, this new brightness, the haircut she'd had over the summer – shorter, jauntier, blonder (they didn't look at all alike: Christina had her father's mousy colouring, his tendency to put on weight, especially around the waist). They'd met for lunch at the Crown, down by Carshalton Ponds, just after she'd had it done. Watching her mother approach, threading her way through the crowded beer garden in her peach slingbacks, Christina had seen her for a moment as others might: an attractive, smiling woman, not the carer, the widow, the one left behind. The thought had cheered her; she'd held her mother to her, told her how wonderful she looked.

'Sounds great, Mum,' she said now. 'Don't worry. We'll find another time. I'd better go. Work, you know.'

'Of course. I'll let you go. Christina?'

'What?'

Another tiny pause. Then, 'You're doing all right, darling, aren't you?'

Christina stared at the spreadsheet, narrowing her eyes until the lines and numbers began to fracture and dissolve. 'Yes, Mum,' she said. 'Really. Don't worry. I'm absolutely fine.'

She stepped out into the garden in the afternoon, retrieved her dad's old rake from the shed. Gardening gloves, her hair scraped back, her ancient kitchen apron on, with its faded blue stripes, its frayed halter attached with safety pins. God knew why she'd kept hold of it; she hated throwing things away, and perhaps that was no bad thing, now that so many of her things – their things – were gone: to storage, to Ed's parents' house, and some, she presumed, to America with him.

Just after three: always, for Christina, the slowest time of day, deadened and dull. It had been different in the office: she'd had distractions then, colleagues, water coolers, tea runs to the canteen. Working from home, there was nothing to leaven the tedium of the client spreadsheets, the expense claims and VAT returns, the emails from panicked theatre directors and gallerists, actors and dancers, asking whether they could expense this dress or that train fare, worrying about whether they were saving enough to pay their tax bill when it came.

Most seemed to wear it almost as a badge of honour, this inability to handle money, the low, rising panic it instilled: *Help us, we are artists, we are not slaves to Mammon.* Jen was impatient with this; she was good with money, she did her self-assessment returns herself, though the broader Arrow Dance finances she left to Christina. Jen's newborn company had been her first client, after university, back when Christina had still had no idea what she wanted to do; she was in recruitment, bored beyond imagining, when Jen had got funding from the Arts Council, founded Arrow Dance, suggested Christina come in to help her with the money side. She'd set up systems, five-year plans, investigated other future sources of financial stability: kept the engine turning over, leaving Jen and her dancers free to think and move and dream. Left recruitment, found other clients in the arts; joined Wright and Marshall, stayed for fifteen years. Gone freelance again three years ago, when it had all got too much: this was after the third round of IVF and the first miscarriage, the one at seven weeks. Their fertility specialist, Dr Ekwensi, had been unable to offer any explanation, just called it one of those terribly unfortunate things. Stress, they'd suspected, she and Ed, stress and long days. And Christina was missing so much work time anyway, what with all the hours they were spending at the clinic, or stuck in traffic getting there and getting home, inching around south London in endless angry rush-hour jams. Patience among the partners at Wright and Marshall had been starting to fray: they had been generous, given her a good severance package. *Stress.* Much better, they'd all agreed, for her to go freelance, establish her own client base again, work from home.

Home. Christina swept, the strokes of the rake rhythmic, soothing. The leaves were dry, friable, easy enough to move from the lawn to the corner of the empty flower bed where she would, she thought, begin a makeshift compost heap, a pile around which she might, one weekend, build wooden sidings. She'd edged the beds herself, not long after they'd moved in:

they'd only taken the flat for the garden, really, which was large for London, for a rented flat, and wild, though Dad had agreed that it had good bones. He'd stood there with her, clutching a mug of tea, surveying the plot while Ed was busy unpacking boxes inside. 'We can clear all this,' Dad had said, sweeping a hand over the scrubby dandelion lawn, the borders choked with nettles and bindweed. 'I'll show you how to edge those borders, neaten them up. It won't take much, Christina – just a few railway sleepers and a bit of elbow grease.'

Right till the end, Dad had looked on the bright side: right till the end, he'd looked for reasons to stay chipper. New treatments, new supplements. Until, in the very last months, when all such approaches had been exhausted, he'd shifted to acceptance. *It's all right, I'm comfortable; I'm ready, I've loved the life I've lived.* Dad's bright, brittle courage, his refusal to fall into despair. She was like him: Mum had always said so; Ed, too. Like Dad, she had refused to fall; like Dad, she had refused to give up.

She stood on the lawn for a moment, rake in hand, breathing, shielding her eyes from the sun. *One last try.* The treatments had cost them so much – their savings, their marriage, everything – but there was still one chance left. Her last chance: it wasn't the same for her as it was for Ed, he had to see that, even now. There had to be a way to reach him – to cut through the layers of exhaustion and resentment, bridge the gulf that had opened up between them, year by year, round by round, until here they were, their marriage over, their possessions divided, their lives five thousand miles apart.

Help us make the next generation of readers

We – both author and publisher – hope you enjoyed this book. We believe that you can become a reader at any time in your life, but we'd love your help to give the next generation a head start.

Did you know that 9 per cent of children don't have a book of their own in their home, rising to 13 per cent in disadvantaged families*? We'd like to try to change that by asking you to consider the role you could play in helping to build readers of the future.

We'd love you to think of sharing, borrowing, reading, buying or talking about a book with a child in your life and spreading the love of reading. We want to make sure the next generation continue to have access to books, wherever they come from.

And if you would like to consider donating to charities that help fund literacy projects, find out more at **www.literacytrust.org.uk** and **www.booktrust.org.uk**.

THANK YOU

*As reported by the National Literacy Trust